Walt Disney's

UNCLE REMUS STORIES

Retold by Marion Palmer

FROM THE ORIGINAL "UNCLE REMUS" STORIES BY

JOEL CHANDLER HARRIS

Pictures by Al Dempster and Bill Justice

ADAPTED FROM THE CHARACTERS AND BACKGROUNDS

CREATED FOR THE

WALT DISNEY

MOTION PICTURE "SONG OF THE SOUTH" AND OTHER

WALT DISNEY ADAPTATIONS OF THE

ORIGINAL "UNCLE REMUS" STORIES

GOLDEN PRESS

NEW YORK

Western Publishing Company, Inc.

Racine, Wisconsin

Contents

PRODUCED IN THE U.S.A. BY WESTERN PUBLISHING COMPANY, INC.

GOLDEN®, A GOLDEN BOOK® and GOLDEN PRESS® are trademarks of Western Publishing Company, Inc.
ISBN 0-307-15551-X

Thirty-fourth Printing, 1982

Foreword

THREE GENERATIONS of readers, young and old, have learned to love the laughter and the wisdom in the tales of Uncle Remus. The pranks of his Brer Rabbit have become a real part of American folklore, so much so that few of us are even aware of the original source from which they came.

Ethnologists agree that the source is quite ancient, that it probably goes back to the legends of the African Negro, long long ago. Slaves brought the legends to this country, and retold them on the old plantations of the South.

It was here in Georgia, in the days of the Civil War, that Joel Chandler Harris first heard them. He listened. With the painstaking care of a scholar, he recorded; he edited; he compiled. Then, with the genius of a true artist, he created his great Negro storyteller, Uncle Remus. It was from the tongue of Uncle Remus in his humble slave cabin that Brer Rabbit, Brer Fox, and all their friends and enemies really came to life. Whether the antics and follies of these creatures would ever have brought such popular enjoyment without Uncle Remus, is hard to say. In any case, Mr. Harris made them immortal, and in Uncle Remus himself he created a character so lovable, so filled with humor and understanding, that he will live as long as literature itself.

It is because of the universal appeal of these legends, and their place in the artistic heritage of this country, that the Disney studio first became interested in presenting them on the screen. During the preparation of material for the motion picture *Song of the South,* a great quantity of the early Remus tales were studied and adapted by the Disney staff. Though we feel that all of them are entertaining and that all of them should be kept alive, we have chosen those we feel to be the most representative for inclusion in this book. We present them here in the hope that the boys and girls of today will chuckle with Brer Rabbit as their parents, their grandparents, and their great grandparents chuckled, long ago.

To those few persons who are familiar with the dialect of the Georgia Negro at the time of the Civil War, it may seem an affront to change in any way the speech of Uncle Remus. Unquestionably, the dialect is a living part of the legends themselves. But after much consideration, we have been forced to conclude that this dialect is much too difficult for the majority of modern, young readers. For this reason, we have greatly simplified it, although with regret that we had to alter it at all.

We do not expect that the stories in this book can take the place of the original Uncle Remus legends. Perhaps, however, they can help to introduce new readers to these legends. There, in the more archaic but picturesque language of the old Negro himself, one may enjoy more fully the rhythm and the poetic fantasy that have made these stories classic.

Walt Disney

Who Was Uncle Remus?

JOHNNY and Uncle Remus were friends. Johnny's hair was brown, his skin was fair, and he was not quite nine. Uncle Remus' hair was white, his skin was black, and no one knew how old he was.

The house where Johnny lived had everything—big rooms, big doors, big doorknobs, big chairs, big windows that looked out on the family's fields of cotton, tobacco, and corn. The cabin where Uncle Remus lived had almost nothing at all, just one little room where Uncle Remus slept and cooked and smoked his corncob pipe. His only window looked out through the trees toward a swamp.

The reason Johnny loved Uncle Remus so much was the wonderful things that he knew. He knew everything there was to know about the birds, the animals, and all the creatures. He even understood the language they used when they spoke; he understood what the Screech-Owl said to the Hoot-Owl in the tree outside his cabin; he understood *I-doom-er-ker-kum-mer-ker*, the Turtle talk, that bubbled up from the bottom of the creek.

Johnny liked to hear Uncle Remus tell stories about what the creatures were doing, and he liked the funny old-fashioned way he spoke. Every evening before supper, he and his friend Ginny went down to Uncle Remus' cabin to listen. All Uncle Remus had to do was to take one puff on his pipe, and a story would just start rolling out with the smoke. It might be a story about a Lion, an Elephant, or a Bullfrog; but most of the stories were about that smartest of all little creatures, Brer Rabbit, and the tricks that he played on Brer Fox and Brer Bear.

"An der will never be an end ter de stories about Brer Rabbit," said Uncle Remus, "cause he's always up ter somethin' new. He ain't very big; he ain't very strong; but when dat thinkin' machine of his starts cookin' up devilment, he's de smartest creetur on dis earf."

De Tar-Baby

ONE DAY, Brer Fox and Brer Bear wuz sittin' round in de woods, talkin' about de way Brer Rabbit wuz always cuttin' up capers an actin' so fresh.

"Brer Rabbit's gettin' too sassy," say Brer Fox.

"Brer Rabbit's gettin' too bossy," say Brer Bear.

"Brer Rabbit don't mind his own bizness," say Brer Fox.

"Brer Rabbit talk too biggity," say Brer Bear.

"I don't like de way Brer Rabbit go prancin' *lippity clippity* down de road," say Brer Bear.

"Some day I'm goin' ter ketch Brer Rabbit an pull out his mustarshes, *pripp! propp!*" say Brer Fox.

"Some day I'm goin' ter ketch Brer Rabbit an knock his head clean off, *blim, blam!*" say Brer Bear.

Right den, Brer Fox get a powerful big idea. "I'm goin' ter ketch Brer Rabbit *now,*" he say.

Well suh, Brer Fox went straight ter wurk. First, he got some tar. Den, he make it inter a shape, sorter like a baby, wid arms and legs, a stummock, an a head. "Now," he say, "we got ter make dis Tar-Baby look real." Wid dat, he pull some hairs, *plip! plip!* right outer Brer Bear's back, and stick um on de Tar-Baby's head. He snatch off Brer Bear's yeller hat an his own blue coat, an he put um on de Tar-Baby. "Come now, Brer Bear," he say, "help me carry dis Tar-Baby ter de big road wher Brer Rabbit's sure ter come hoppin' along."

Dey took de Tar-Baby, and dey sot him down under a tree at de side of de road, sorter like he mighter been restin'. Den, Brer Fox an Brer Bear lay down in de bushes ter wait fer Brer Rabbit.

Dey didn't have ter wait long. Purty soon, dey heard a whistlin' an a hummin', an along come Brer Rabbit prancin' *lippity clippity,* sassy ez a mockin' bird. All 't once, he spy de Tar-Baby.

"Howdy!" sing out Brer Rabbit.

De Tar-Baby, he say nothin', an Brer Fox an Brer Bear, dey lay low in de bushes an dey say nothin'.

Brer Rabbit wait fer de Tar-Baby ter answer. Den he say, louder dan before, "What's de matter wid you? I said *howdy do.* Is you deaf? If you is, I can holler louder."

De Tar-Baby, he say nothin', an Brer Fox an Brer Bear, dey lay low.

Den Brer Rabbit holler at de Tar-Baby loud ez he can. "Wher's your politeness? Ain't you goin' ter say *howdy* like respectubble folks say when dey meet up on de road?"

De Tar-baby, he say nothin', an Brer Fox an Brer Bear, dey lay low.

Now Brer Rabbit sorter mad. He clinch his fist and he walk right up close ter de Tar-Baby. "If you don't say *howdy* by de time I count three, I'm goin' ter blip you in de nose." Brer Rabbit start countin', "One, two, . . ."

But de Tar-Baby, he say nothin', an Brer Fox and Brer Bear, dey just wink der eyes an grin.

"Three!" yell Brer Rabbit. Now he mighty mad. He draw back his fist, an *blip!* he hit de Tar-Baby smack in de nose. But Brer Rabbit's fist stuck der in de tar. He can't pull it loose.

Now Brer Rabbit turrible mad. "Let go my fist!" he holler. Wid dat, he draw back his other fist, and *blip!* again he hit de Tar-Baby smack in de nose. But dis fist stuck der in de tar too. He can't pull it loose.

De Tar-Baby, he say nothin', an Brer Fox an Brer Bear dey sorter chuckle in der stummocks.

"If you don't let go my fists," holler Brer Rabbit, "I'm goin' ter kick your teef right outer your mouf!"

Well suh, Brer Rabbit kicked. First he pull back one behind foot, an *pow!* he hit de Tar-Baby in de jaw. But Brer Rabbit's behind foot stuck der in de tar. Den, *pow!* he hit de Tar-Baby wid de other behind foot. Dis foot stuck der in de tar too.

"If you don't let go my behind foots," squall out Brer Rabbit, "I'm goin' ter butt you wid my head till you ain't got no bref left in your body!"

Brer Rabbit butted, but his head stuck der in de tar. Now Brer Rabbit's two fists, his two behind foots, an his head wuz all stuck in de Tar-Baby. He push an he pull, but de more he try ter get unstuck-up, de stucker-up he got. Soon Brer Rabbit is so stuck up he can't skacely move his eyeballs.

Now Brer Fox an Brer Bear come outer de bushes, an dey feel mighty good. Dey dance round an round Brer Rabbit, laffin' and hollerin' fit ter kill.

"We sure ketched you dis time, Brer Rabbit," say Brer Bear.

"You better say your prayers, Brer Rabbit," say Brer Fox, "cause dis is de very last day of your life."

Brer Rabbit, he shiver an trimble, cause he wuz in a mighty bad fix, an he wuz mighty skeered. But right den he set his mind a-workin' how ter get hisself outer dat fix real quick.

"Brer Rabbit," say Brer Bear, "you been bouncin' round dis neighborhood bossin' everybody fer a long time. Now I'm de boss, an I'm goin' ter knock your head clean off."

"No," say Brer Fox. "Dat's too easy an too quick. We got ter make him suffer."

"Brer Rabbit," he say, "you been sassin' me, stickin' your head inter my bizness fer years an years. Now I got you. I'm goin' ter fix up a great big fire. Den, when it's good an hot, I'm goin' ter drop you in an roast you, right here dis very day."

Now Brer Rabbit ain't really skeered any more, cause he got an idea how he goin' ter get loose. But he talk like he's de most skeered rabbit in all dis wurld. "I don't care what you do wid me," he say, pretendin' ter shake an quake all over, "just so you don't fling me over dese bushes into dat brier-patch. Roast me just ez hot ez you please, but don't fling me in dat brier-patch!"

"Hold on a minute," say Brer Bear, tappin' Brer Fox on de shoulder. "It's goin' ter be a lot of trouble ter roast Brer Rabbit. Furst, we'll have ter fetch a big pile of kindlin' wood."

Brer Fox scratch his head. "Dat's so. Well den, Brer Rabbit, I'm goin' ter hang you."

"Hang me just ez high ez you please," say Brer Rabbit, "but please don't fling me in dat brier-patch!"

"It's goin' ter be a lot of trouble ter hang Brer Rabbit," say Brer Bear. "Furst, we'll have ter fetch a big long rope."

"Dat's so," say Brer Fox. "Well den, Brer Rabbit, I'm goin' ter drown you."

"Drown me just ez deep ez you please," say

Brer Rabbit, "but please, *please* don't fling me in dat brier-patch!"

"It's goin' ter be a lot of trouble ter drown Brer Rabbit," say Brer Bear. "Furst, we'll have ter carry him way down to de river."

"Dat's so," say Brer Fox. "Well, Brer Rabbit, I expect de best way is ter skin you. Come on, Brer Bear, let's get started."

"Skin me," say Brer Rabbit, "pull out my ears, snatch off my legs an chop off my tail, but please, *please,* PLEASE, Brer Fox an Brer Bear, *don't* fling me in dat brier-patch!"

Now Brer Bear sorter grumble. "Wait a minute, Brer Fox. It ain't goin' ter be much fun ter skin Brer Rabbit, cause he ain't skeered of bein' skinned."

"But he sure *is* skeered of dat brier-patch!" say Brer Fox. "An dat's just wher he's goin' ter go! Dis is de end of Brer Rabbit!" Wid dat, he yank Brer Rabbit off de Tar-Baby an he fling him, *kerblam!* right inter de middle of de brier-patch.

Well suh, der wuz a considerabul flutter in de place where Brer Rabbit struck dose brier-bushes. "*Ooo! Oow! Ouch!*" he yell. He screech an he squall. De ruckus an de hullabaloo wuz awful. Den, by-m-by, de *Ooo* and de *Oow* an de *Ouch* come only in a weak tired whisper, like Brer Rabbit really goin' ter die.

Brer Fox and Brer Bear, dey listen an grin. Den dey shake hands an dey slap each other on de back.

"Brer Rabbit ain't goin' ter be sassy no more!"

"Brer Rabbit ain't goin' ter be bossy no more!"

"Brer Rabbit ain't goin' ter do *nothin'* no more!"

"Dis is de end! *Brer Rabbit is dead!*"

But right den, Brer Fox an Brer Bear hear a scufflin' mongst de leaves, way at de other end of de brier-patch. And lo an behold, who do dey see scramblin' out from de bushes, frisky ez a cricket, but Brer Rabbit hisself! *Brer Rabbit,* whistlin' an singin', an combin' de last bit of tar outer his mustarshes wid a piece of de brier-bush!

"Howdy, Brer Fox an Brer Bear!" he holler. "I told you an I told you not to fling me in dat brier-patch. Dat's de place in all dis world I love de very best. Dat brier-patch is de place wher I wuz born!"

Wid dat, he prance away, *lippity-clippity,* laffin' an laffin' till he can't laff no more.

13

Brer Terrapin's Tug-of-War

ONE NIGHT, de creeturs dat lived in Brer Rabbit's neighborhood decided ter ferget der quarrels, an meet tergedder fer a taffy-pull down by de pond. 'Twuz a moonshiny night when all de stars wuz twinklin' and everybody wuz feelin' fine.

Everybody wanted ter help. Brer Bear, he fetched de wood. Brer Fox, he built de fire. Brer Wolf, he come along wid de stew pot ter cook de taffy. Miss Possum, she bring a big spoon ter stir it, an Miss Mink, she bring a little spoon ter taste it when 'twuz done. Ez fer Brer Rabbit, he grease de bottom of de plates ter keep de taffy from stickin'. Den Brer Terrapin, he climb up on a rock, an say he'd watch an see dat de pot don't boil over.

Well . . . whiles dey wuz all sittin' round, an de taffy wuz a-boilin' an a-bubblin', dey got ter tellin' tales. Soon, dey got ter braggin'.

Brer Fox, he start it up. "Folks," he brag, "I wanter say right here an now, dat of all de creeturs in dis wurld, I am de sharpest."

"Haw!" say Brer Wolf. "Maybe you is de sharpest, but I'm de wickedest."

"An I'm de prettiest," say Miss Mink, swishin' her little brown tail.

"An I'm de spryest," say Miss Possum, swingin' herself upside down from a tree branch.

14

"Pooh!" say Brer Bear. "Who cares about all dat?" He snort an puff out his big furry chest. "I'm de strongest!"

Brer Rabbit, he lissen ter all de braggin', an he say ter hisself, "Dese creeturs talk too biggity, exceptin' my friend little Brer Terrapin, an he don't talk biggity at all." Dis set Brer Rabbit ter thinkin', an purty soon his head wuz full of devilment. By-m-by, when nobody wuz lookin', he sorter mosey up ter Brer Terrapin. Dey whisper together fer a while. Den, dey bof grin, an Brer Rabbit, he mosey off again.

Brer Terrapin wait fer a bit. Den, he stick his head way outer his shell, an he say, "Who wuz dat who say he is de strongest?"

"Dat wuz me," say Brer Bear, struttin' an puffin' his chest out again. "Does anybody say I *ain't* de strongest?"

"Yes," say Brer Terrapin. "I do. You ain't de strongest. I is."

Dis make all de creeturs chuckle and giggle, cause of course Brer Terrapin ain't much bigger dan de palm of Brer Bear's paw. Brer Bear, he roll on de ground an laff and laff. After a while, he pick hisself up, an he say, sorter snickerin', "Come, Brer Terrapin, you say you is de strongest. How you goin' ter prove it?"

"What'll you give me if I prove it?" ask Brer Terrapin.

Now Brer Rabbit wink his eye at Brer Terrapin, an he speak up. "Look here, folks . . . if dis little Terrapin can prove he stronger dan big Brer Bear, we ought ter give him a hansome present. We ought ter give him all de taffy dat's boilin' in dis here pot!"

"Dat's right!" holler all de creeturs, chucklin'. Natchally, dey know Brer Bear is de strongest.

"Very well," say Brer Bear, "it's agreed. Brer Terrapin gets all de taffy in de pot if he can prove he is de strongest. Now Brer Terrapin, how you goin' ter prove it?"

"Get me a big, long rope," say Brer Terrapin. "I'll take one end, an crawl down inter de pond. You take de other end, an see if you strong enuff ter pull me out."

"I ain't got no rope," say Brer Bear.

"You ain't got no rope, an you ain't got no strength, either." Brer Terrapin pull back inter his shell, like he got nothin' more ter say.

Brer Bear an de others, dey just laff, but Brer Rabbit, he up an say, "Dis argument got ter be settled right now. We got ter know who is de strongest."

Wid dat, ne skip away, an before you can say *hoop-dee-doo*, back he come, draggin' a big long rope. One end of it, he give ter Brer Bear. De other end, he give ter Brer Terrapin.

"Now, ladies and gentermens," he say, "you all just stay here wid Brer Bear. I'll step down ter de edge of de pond wid Brer Terrapin. Soon ez I see him crawl down under de water, an it's time fer Brer Bear ter pull, I'll wave an holler, 'Woop!'"

Well suh, dey all laff again, but dey do ez dey wuz told. Brer Rabbit, he grin ter hisself when he see Brer Terrapin take his end of de rope an dive down inter de pond. Down he go, *kerblink, kerblunk!* way down ter de very bottom.

Brer Rabbit wait a minute. Den he holler inter de water, "Is you ready, Brer Terrapin?"

Brer Terrapin, he send up a bubble dat say Yes. Now Brer Rabbit wave ter Brer Bear an de other creeturs, an he holler, "*Woop!*"

De tug-of-war begin. Brer Bear, he wrap de rope round one paw, an give it a little jerk. But Brer Terrapin, he don't budge. De creeturs standin' der wid Brer Bear, dey open up der eyes cause dey sorter puzzled.

Den Brer Bear, he take de rope in bof paws, an give it a bigger jerk. But Brer Terrapin, he don't budge. De creeturs, dey frown, cause now dey really puzzled.

Brer Bear try again. Dis time he put de rope 'cross his shoulder. He lean forerd an grunt, an

he pull wid all his might. Brer Terrapin, he don't budge. He send up another bubble.

"He wants ter know when you're goin' ter start pullin'," holler Brer Rabbit. He laff ter hisself. Den he wrinkle up his nose ter sniff de sweetness of de taffy a-bubblin' in de pot.

Now, de creeturs gettin' kinder worried. Brer Fox, he step up an grab hold of de rope ter help Brer Bear. Dey bof pull. Dey pull an dey pull, till dey ain't got bref ter pull any more. But Brer Terrapin, he just send up a bubble.

"He says he's gettin' tired of waitin'," holler Brer Rabbit. "What's de matter, Brer Bear? Ain't you got no strength?"

Now de creeturs turrible worried, cause dey remember de promise dey made 'bout de taffy. Dey all grab hold of de rope ter help Brer Bear, an dey all pull tergedder. Dey pull an dey pull. Dey pull till dey so tired dey can't stand on der foots. Den dey just let go.

Of course, all dis while Brer Terrapin had his end of de rope tied on ter an old tree stump a-growin' on de bottom of de pond. All he had ter do wuz just sit der in de mud, twiddlin' his thumbs. Soon ez he see dat de rope ain't pullin' on de stump no more, he know dat Brer Bear give up. Den he untie de rope, an up he swim ter de top of de water. By de time de other creeturs come down ter de edge of de pond, Brer Terrapin wuz just strollin' round, stretchin' his neck, an gazin' at de stars.

"Dat last pull of yours wuz purty stiff, Brer Bear," he say. "You're strong, you're mighty strong, but you just ain't strong enuff!" Brer Terrapin grin. "Now if you'll please excuse me, I'll take de taffy an go on along home. Come on, Brer Rabbit, give me a hand wid carryin' dat great big pot."

Wid dat, Brer Rabbit an Brer Terrapin picked up de pot of taffy an took it home ter der chilluns, an not one of de other creeturs got so much ez a teenchy little taste.

16

Brer Bear an de Bag Full of Turkeys

ONE DAY, Brer Rabbit wuz loungin' round under a pomegranate tree, puzzlin' what he wuz goin' ter do next. He just can't make up his mind. On de one hand, he wuz feelin' sorter hongry, but on de other hand, he wuz feelin' sorter lazy, an he ain't in de mood ter scurry round an fetch hisself somethin' ter eat.

By-m-by, he seed Brer Bear come along wid a big empty bag slung over his shoulder. "Howdy, Brer Bear! Wher you goin' wid dat bag?"

"I'm goin' huntin' So long!" Wid dat Brer Bear go trudgin' off on his way.

Brer Rabbit grin. Now he know dat he ain't goin' ter be hongry too long; an on de other hand, he know dat he don't have ter scurry round an fetch hisself somethin' ter eat.

Well suh, de rest of de day, till de time dat de sun dropped down, Brer Rabbit just puff on his pipe an loll around. Den he get up, an he climb up in a tree ter watch fer Brer Bear ter come back from his huntin'. He ain't been watchin' very long when, sure enuff, he seed Brer Bear come trompin' throo de woods wid his huntin'-bag filled up wid turkeys.

Brer Rabbit jump down from de tree. He scamper throo de bushes, an he come out at a place on de road wher Brer Bear wuz bound ter pass by. Den he set ter wurk. Furst, he pull a twig off one of de bushes. He take out his knife,

17

an he cut de twig inter de shape of an arrow. Next, he take off his clothes, an he hide um der in de tall grass. Of course, widout his own shirt, an widout his own pants, an widout his own pipe, Brer Rabbit don't look like Brer Rabbit at all. He look like any other ordinary rabbit in de wurld.

Now Brer Rabbit lay down on de ground, an he put de arrow against his side, lookin' like't wuz stuck right throo his heart. Den he stretch out straight an stiff, exactly like he wuz dead.

Purty soon, along come Brer Bear. When he seed a rabbit layin' der on de ground wid a arrow stickin' throo him, he stop an take a look.

"Mmmm," he say ter hisself, "somebody must have shot dis rabbit. Mmm . . . mmm, such a fine, fat rabbit! He sure looks mighty tasty!" Brer Bear sorter lick his chops. Den he look down at his huntin'-bag, filled up so full wid turkeys. "Too bad I ain't got room ter put dis rabbit in der! Oh well, I ain't!" He sigh, an tromp on down de road.

Soon ez Brer Bear wuz outer sight, up jump Brer Rabbit. Off he scamper throo de woods, an

come out at another place on de road wher Brer Bear wuz bound ter pass by. Again he lay down on de ground. Again he put de arrow against his side, an stretch out like he wuz dead.

By-m-by, along come Brer Bear. "My, my!" he say. "Another rabbit! An just ez fat ez de first one!" He look at Brer Rabbit a minute, an his mouf begin ter water. Den he sling his bag of turkeys down from his shoulder, an drop it on de ground. "Dese fat rabbits is goin' ter waste. I can't allow dat. I'll just leave my turkeys here a minute, while I go back an fetch dat other rabbit. Den I'll string de two rabbits tergedder, an I'll just drag um de rest of de way home."

Wid dat, Brer Bear marched back down de road toward de place wher he seed de first rabbit.

Skacely wuz Brer Bear outer sight, when Brer Rabbit jump up. He grab de bag full of turkeys, an off he prance *lippity-clippity,* grinnin' an chucklin' an laffin' big laffs.

An Brer Bear went home widout his turkeys, an widout his two fat rabbits, an he never did find out who stole um.

Doctor Rabbit Cures de King

ER COME a time when King Lion got a brier stuck in his paw, an he got sorter sick. Day after day, he sot der on his throne, a-groanin' an a-groanin', skace able ter hold de crown on his head.

De creeturs dat he wuz a-kingin' over, dey had ter scratch round ter fetch him his food. An dis wan't no easy matter, fer King Lion had a appetite bigger dan a Hippytamypottymus. It got so dat after a while, every fambly had ter share der dinner wid de King, ter keep him from starvin' ter deff.

De Lion-Doctor, he try ter cure de King's paw, but he can't. Den somebody whisper in King Lion's ear dat der wuz a heap of smartness mongst de creeturs dat he kinged over, an maybe he ought ter inquire round 'bout some smart new doctor. First thing you know, de King wuz sendin' inquirements out, an purty soon dey tell him 'bout Brer Rabbit. Of course, dey say, Brer Rabbit ain't a reg'lar doctor wid a sachel of powders an pills, but he do have some herbs an erntments dat he got from de Witch-Rabbit down in de swamp.

De next thing you know, de King send fer Brer Rabbit, an he come a-runnin' ter see what he can do. Now ter look at de paw dat de brier wuz stuck in, Brer Rabbit had ter go mighty close ter King Lion's mouf. He didn't like dat kinder bizness. Every time he'd feel de hot breff of King Lion blowin' on him, he'd flinch an squinch all up. An when King Lion yawned,

Brer Rabbit well-nigh fainted dead away. Howsomever, he did de best he could. He fixed up de paw wid a salve of turkentime an suet, ter draw de infermation out. He tell de King he goin' ter get better, an den he say "So long."

Now Brer Rabbit mosey off down de road a bit, just whistlin' an singin' a silly, sassy chune. By-m-by, he meet Brer Fox, hurryin' along wid a pair of fat ducks fer his share of de King's dinner.

Brer Rabbit, he howdy'd.

Brer Fox, he hello'd, an den he ask, "By de way, Dr. Rabbit, how's de King? Better?"

Brer Rabbit rub his chin an look sorter wise. "Well, he is, an den again, he isn't. It all depends on what he puts in his stummock."

"Den I'll be de one ter cure him!" Brer Fox fro out his chest. He look round at de two fat

ducks strung over his shoulder, an he give um a little pat. "You know how de King loves ducks!"

"Oh gracious! Oh goodness!" Brer Rabbit drop his mouf wide open. "Why, what a piece of luck dat I met up wid you dis way! You musn't take dose ducks ter King Lion, oh no!"

"Why not?" ask Brer Fox. "Dese is fine ducks! Dey'll make de King feel better in a jiffy!"

Brer Rabbit laff way down in his insides, but he don't let on. "No, Brer Fox, de King likes ducks, but he can't have um. Dey'll make him awful sick! I'm de Doctor, an I know. If you don't believe my say-so, just look here." Brer Rabbit feel round in his pocket an pull out a little piece of old newspaper.

Brer Fox look at it kinder sideways. "Is der any writin' on it? If der is, 't ain't goin' ter do me no good ter look at it. I can read readin', but I can't read writin'."

"Dat's de way wid me too," say Brer Rabbit, "exceptin' dat I can read writin' but I can't read readin'." Den he kinder wrinkle up his forehead an look down at de paper like it say somethin'. "Dis is writin', Brer Fox, an I'll be glad ter read it ter you. Here's what it say:

'Dese is de foods dat King Lion may eat— hot meat, cold meat, fresh meat, stale meat —any kinder meat at all, exceptin' DUCK meat, an dat's sure ter give him chills an fever.' "

"Chills an fever! Den I can't take him dese ducks!" Now Brer Fox look sorter skeered. "But what am I goin' ter do, Brer Rabbit? Now I ain't got nothin' ter take him fer his dinner! Oh . . . oh . . . he'll be turrible mad! What *will* I do?"

"You're in a bad fix, Brer Fox, mighty bad!" Brer Rabbit scratch his ear wid his behind foot, like he thinkin' real hard. Den he say, "If I wuz you, I'd just take dose ducks home ter Mrs. Fox. Den I'd run off somewhers an hide—somewhers way off, far far away, so's King Lion can't send no one ter ketch you."

"Dat's just what I'll do! Thankee, Brer Rabbit!" Wid dat, Brer Fox tear off down de road like he been shot from a cannon.

Soon ez he got outer sight, Brer Rabbit sot down on his hunkers an had a big laff. Den, when he know dat de time wuz long enuff fer Brer Fox ter get home wid de ducks, an be off again, he foller along ter Brer Fox's house.

He step up ter de door an he rap on it, soft— *blim!* He stand der, wid his heels tergedder, lookin' like really-truly goodness wuz just drippin' from his mouf.

Mrs. Fox, she open de door, an Brer Rabbit, he make a bow. "Good evenin', Mrs. Fox. I hope you is feelin' well." Den he sorter pull his mustarshes an scrape his foot on de step. "I wuz just a-passin' by, an if you don't mind, I'll take along dose two ducks Brer Fox done give me dis mawnin'."

Mrs. Fox, she put her hands on her hips an she look monstrus cross. "Well, well, well! If dat don't beat everything! Dat scallywag Fox of mine! He up an give you dose ducks an he don't say nothin' ter me about it!"

"Why, dat's too bad, Mrs. Fox, but see, here 'tis in writin' dat de ducks is mine." Brer Rabbit

take out de same little piece of newspaper dat he showed ter Brer Fox, an hold it up fer Mrs. Fox ter see. Mrs. Fox, she turn it upperside-downside an wrongside-outside. Den she say she can't read it widout her far-seein' specks. She hand it back ter Brer Rabbit ter read aloud.

Brer Rabbit, he clear his throat, an make out dat he readin':

" 'Dearest Wife: Pleased be so kind ez ter let Brer Rabbit take de two ducks. Your lovin' Fox.' "

"Well," say Mrs. Fox, kinder grittin' her teef, "I guess dey's yours." She fetch de two ducks an hand um ter Brer Rabbit.

"Thankee, Mrs. Fox," say Brer Rabbit, bowin' an takin' de ducks. Wid dat, he light out from der, an away he gallop home. Dat night, de Rabbit fambly ate dose ducks fer dinner—all exceptin' de gizzards, an dose Mrs. Rabbit cooked up speshal fer Brer Rabbit ter take ter de King. An dat very day after dinner, King Lion got well, cause der ain't nothin' on dis earf so tasty ter a sick Lion ez de gizzards of fine, fat ducks.

Why de Cricket Fambly Lives in Chimbleys

ONCE UPON A TIME—it might have been in de year One, fer all I know—der wuz a frisky young Cricket dat liked ter play on his fife. All durin' de summer, he'd stay out in de woods, an one day he'd fife fer de fishes, an de next he'd teach de young birds how ter whistle a chune. Day in an day out, he frolicked an had fun, but by-m-by, de weather began ter get cool. Den playin' de fife wuz difficult bizness. All mawnin' while de frost nipped round, dis frisky young Cricket had ter keep his hands in his pockets ter keep his joints from stiffen' up.

Dis wuz bad enuff, but it kept on gettin' wuss. It got so cold dat Mr. Cricket can't play his fife at all. He had ter tuck his fife up under his arm, while he just shivered an huddled up mongst de stones. Now he know dat somethin' just had ter be done.

So he crawl along throo de woods, till after a while, he seed a house wid some smoke a-risin' from a chimbley at de back. "Ah-ha!" he say ter hisself. "Wher der's smoke, der's bound ter be a fire. Der I can get warm." He creep up close, an he seed dat de house wuz made of logs, an de chimbley just plain mud, plastered on some sticks. Mr. Cricket smile, cause dis wuz de kind of chimbley dat wuz easy ter get inter.

He set ter work. He gnawed an he sawed, he scratched an he clawed, an purty soon, he got wher he could feel some warmf. More dan dat, der wuz some cracks in de hearf of de fireplace

23

inside de house, an some crumbs had fallen throo. Mr. Cricket smelt um, an felt um, an ate um, an after dat, he wuz feelin' fine.

'Twan't long before his joints go soople again, so he took out his fife an begun ter play. In de daytime, he played real softly, but when de nighttime come, an everythin' wuz dark, he played ez loud ez he can. De chillun in de house, dey lissen an laff, but de mammy an de daddy dey shake der heads an look sorter cross.

Day after day, an night after night, de fifin' went on.

After a while, de daddy begun ter get mad. "Stop dat racket!" he holler down throo de crack in de hearf.

But de fifin' went on.

De daddy stomp an shake his fist. "Hush up! You hush up or I'll make you sorry!"

But de fifin' went on.

Now de daddy too mad fer ter speak. He up an put de kettle on de fire an wait till de water boil. Den, whiles de fifin' wuz de loudest, he

took an poured de scaldin' water down throo de cracks in de hearf. De next thing dat daddy know, he know he shouldn't have done it, cause de water melted de mud an plaster, an de hearf fell in. De hearf fallin' in pulled de chimbley down. De chimbley fallin' down pulled de wall down. De wall fallin' down pulled de roof down, an de daddy an de mammy an de chilluns had ter run out from der ruint house inter de woods.

Mr. Cricket, he kicked an pushed an shoved an scrooged, till he got out from de place wher de chimbley wuz. But de weather outside wuz cold. He had ter put his hands in his pockets, an he can't fife. So he went on ter de next house, an crawled in de chimbley der.

But de daddy an de mammy an de chilluns didn't have no place ter crawl inter. Dey had ter make der beds in de trees. So dey called out ter der friends ter tell *der* friends, an fer *dem* ter tell der friends' friends, not ter pour boilin' water on de crickets in der chimbleys, else der houses would be ruint. An dat's why de Cricket fambly been livin' in chimbleys from dat day down ter dis, an no one dasn't disturb um.

24

Brer Rabbit Rides de Fox

MISS GOOSE wuz goin' ter have a birf-day party.

All de creeturs in de neighbor-hood wuz invited. Dey wuz asked ter put on der Sunday clothes, an dey wuz expected ter behave wid der Sunday manners, like one big fambly. 'Twuz understood dat der would be no growlin', bitin', snarlin' nor snappin'.

De mawnin' of dat party, Brer Rabbit jump outer bed real early, an start ter primp up. He koam up his hair an his ears. He twist his mus-tarshes. He brush de cockle-burrs outer his tail. Den he look in his lookin'-glass. He wink one eye at hisself an grin, cause he know he goin' ter be de fanciest, dandiest creetur at de party.

Brer Rabbit put on his hat, an he start ter de door, but just den, he hear a rustlin' in de leaves outside. "Hmm" . . . he say, hoistin' up his ears. He tiptoe ter de winder, easy-like, an peek out. Lo an behold, what does he see stickin' out from behind de sic'more tree, but de tip end of Brer Fox tail! "Oh ho!" he say. "Dat Fox is up ter somethin', an he ain't up ter no good." Brer Rab-bit peek some more an he seed dat Brer Fox wuz all slicked up, an wearin' his best party pants.

Now Brer Rabbit start thinkin'. "Dat Fox is jealous, dat's what he is. He don't want me ter go ter dat party. He's goin' ter act like we're friends, an like we oughter go ter Miss Goose house tergedder. But he's got some plan ter do away wid me before we get der, sure ez my name's Rabbit. Hmmmm, well, I got a plan too."

An right den, Brer Rabbit put his plan ter wurk. He lay down on de floor close by de door, an he begin ter moan. "O-o-o-o-o, O-w-w-w, O-o-o-o, I so sick! O-o-o, I so sick!"

Outside, Brer Fox lissen. He frown. He wuz-zent expectin' ter find Brer Rabbit sick, an dis kinder put kinks in his plan. By-m-by, he step up ter de door an knock . . . *blim!*

Brer Rabbit moan some more, "O-o-o, O-w-w, who's dat knockin' at my door?"

"It's your good friend Brer Fox. I come ter take you ter Miss Goose party."

"Thankee, Brer Fox, but I'm too sick ter go."

"Ah, come on, Brer Rabbit. You'll be all right. Maybe you'll feel better soon."

"Oh no, Brer Fox, I'm very, very sick! O-o-o, O-o-o!"

Now Brer Fox don't know what ter do. He pace up an down outside de door, puzzlin' an wurkin' his mind. Brer Rabbit's bein' sick has spoilt everything. "I just got ter do away wid him somehow," he say ter hisself. "If only I can get him ez far ez de bridge dat crosses de river, den I can fling him in! Bein' ez he's so sick, he's sure ter drown quick." Brer Fox grin. "But first, I got ter get him ter come out."

Brer Fox step up ter de door an knock again, *blam!* "You *got* ter come ter de party, Brer Rab-bit," he say, real perlite. "It just won't seem de same widout you."

"But I can't come, Brer Fox. I can't skacely even walk!"

"Dat don't matter, Brer Rabbit. If you is too

25

sick ter walk, I'll carry you. I'll be glad ter. I'll carry you in my arms."

Dis make Brer Rabbit chuckle, cause now he know dat his plan goin' ter wurk. "Thankee, Brer Fox," he say, "dat's mighty nice of you ter say you'll carry me, but I'm skeered you'll drop me. O-o-o. O-o-o. I'm so sick!"

"I won't drop you, Brer Rabbit, but if you're skeered, well, I'll let you ride on my back."

"Thankee, Brer Fox, but I'm skeered I'll fall off. I can't ride widout a saddle. I'm a very sick Rabbit!"

Brer Fox don't like de idea of puttin' on a saddle, but he got ter get Brer Rabbit outer dat house, else he can't get him ter de river ter drown him. He grit his teef. "I'll be glad ter put on a saddle," he say.

Now Brer Rabbit groan like he feelin' wurse. "I'm a turrible sick Rabbit, Brer Fox, an I don't want you shyin' at somethin' an throwin' me off on de road. A saddle ain't enuff. I got ter have a bridle too."

Dis make Brer Fox mighty mad, but he want ter get Brer Rabbit outer dat house mighty bad. He take a deep bref, an he say, "I'll be pleased ter put on a bridle, Brer Rabbit, but you can ride me only ez far ez de bridge dat crosses de river. Dat's de gettin'-off-place, an you got ter walk

26

de rest of de way ter de party on your own feet."

Now Brer Fox grin wide, cause he know de bridge is de place wher he goin' ter fling Brer Rabbit *kerjoom!* down inter de deep, deep water.

"Dat'll be just fine. I'll get off der," say Brer Rabbit. "I sure is obliged ter you, Brer Fox. Maybe I won't be feelin' so sick by de time we get ter de river."

Well, Brer Fox, he scamper off ter get hisself harnessed up.

Brer Rabbit, he scramble up from de floor, an what does he do but go ter de shelf, take down a pair of spurs, an slip dem inter his pocket! Den, he pick up his banjo, an a bouquet of blubby-blossoms dat he had fixed up fer Miss Goose. Last of all, he wrap hisself up in a big flannil blanket ter make hisself look powerful sick.

By-m-by, he hear Brer Fox come gallopin' back. Brer Rabbit go out.

Der wuz Brer Fox a-standin' der waitin', sad-

dled, bridled, an all rigged up like a circus pony! "Come on, Brer Rabbit," he holler, "let's get goin'. Take off dat blanket an climb up."

"I got ter wear dis blanket," say Brer Rabbit, shiverin' a little. "I can't afford ter ketch cold." Wid dat, he slowly hoist hisself up inter de saddle. "Now go easy wid me, Brer Fox. I'm a very sick rabbit."

Brer Fox trot off. Brer Rabbit, he just sot der in de saddle, jouncin', bouncin', an moanin' an groanin' like he feel wurser an wurser all de time. Brer Fox smack his lips. He can't skacely wait ter get ter de bridge over de river, wher he goin' ter fling Brer Rabbit an drown him.

Well suh, he trot an he trot, an after a while, he get der. Brer Fox stop still. "Here we is, Brer Rabbit. Dis is de gettin'-off-place. Climb down." Brer Fox lissen ter de gurglin' of de water down under de bridge, an he chuckle.

Brer Rabbit, he twist an turn in de saddle, like he startin' ter get down, but of course, he wan't doin' nothin' but pullin' his spurs outer his pocket an slippin' dem over his foots.

"Just a minute, Brer Fox, just wait till I get loose from dis here blanket!"

"Hurry, Brer Rabbit, hurry up!" Brer Fox just can't wait. He paw up de ground an he chomp at de bit.

"Just a minute, Brer Fox, just a minute!"

Now Brer Rabbit ready. He fling off de blanket. He fro out his chest. "*Giddyap!*" he yell. Den he lift up his heels, an *grrrpp!* down splunge de spurs right inter Brer Fox ribs!

"Oow! Ouch!" squall Brer Fox. He rip 'n roar! He jump an hump, but every time he hump his-

self, Brer Rabbit just slap de spurs in him harder.

Brer Fox snort. Den up he leap an away he gallop, *lickity-splickity!*

Brer Rabbit, he wave his hat. "Yippee! Yippee!" he holler. He ride dat Fox just like a cowboy. He drive him right up ter de gate of Miss Goose house.

De creeturs der at de party come crowdin' ter de door. "It's Brer Rabbit!" dey shout. "Look! Why, bless gracious! He's ridin' Brer Fox!"

Brer Rabbit, he drive Brer Fox right up onter de peazzer. Den he lean down an make a bow, an hand Miss Goose de bouquet of blubby-blossoms.

"Howdy, folks!" he say. "Now please excuse me just a second while I tie up my ridin' hoss!"

Wid dat, he jump down from Brer Fox an tie him up fast ter de post. Ole Brer Fox so tired his tongue wuz out, his tail wuz droopin' down, an he ain't got no bref fer ter speak.

Den Brer Rabbit grab up his banjo, an he prance right inter de party, strummin' an singin' a song:

"*Some folks travels fancy*
  Some folks travels plain,
  Some folks goes on hoss-back,
    Others takes de train.
  Some folks has a carriage
    Wid a coachman on de box,
      but—
  When I goes ter a party
    I travels on ole Brer Fox."

Brer Fox an de Stolen Goobers

DER WUZ one season when Brer Fox took a notion ter plant a goober patch. "Now when dese goobers is ripe," he say ter hisself, "dey's goin' ter be mine, all mine, an nobody else is goin' ter get um." Wid dat, he fetch some boards, an he build a big high fence all de way round wher de goobers wuz planted.

By-m-by, de goobers begin ter ripen up, an Brer Fox go down ter pick um. But lo an be-hold, he find dat somebody else has picked um first.

Brer Fox mad. "Somebody's been a-grabblin' mongst my vines," he say, mutterin' an shakin' his fists. He walk round an round de goober patch, lookin' for dat somebody's tracks, but he can't find um. "Dat villyun's smart, whomsoever he is, mighty smart," he say. "I'll bet it's dat rabbit, dat's who 'tis, it's Brer Rabbit!"

Now Brer Fox begin huntin' everywher fer de

crawl throo de hole. *Pow!* De loop-knot ketch him just behind his little front paws. *Whoop!* Up flew'd de tree branch, an der wuz Brer Rabbit high up in de air, danglin' 'twixt de heavens an de earf! An der he swung. First he feared he goin' ter fall. Den he feared he wuzzent goin' ter fall. He yank an pull, an he heave an he haul, but 't ain't no use. Dis time, he know Brer Fox got him ketched.

Whilst he wuz swingin' up der, figgerin' out a way ter get loose, he hear somebody trompin' down de road. Presently, along come Brer Bear. Now Brer Rabbit begin ter feel better.

"Howdy, Brer Bear," he sing out.

Brer Bear turn round. "Huh?" Den he see Brer Rabbit hangin' down from de tree on de rope. "Heyo, Brer Rabbit, what you doin' up der?"

"Who? Me? Oh, I'm just—just wurkin' on a job."

"*Wurkin' on a job!*" Brer Bear scratch his

place in de fence wher Brer Rabbit come in. Brer Fox eyes mighty sharp, an purty soon he seed a hole wher de wood had been sorter chewed off. He grin. "Hmmmm, dis is de place Brer Rabbit comes in, right here! An dis is de place wher I'll ketch him when he comes back."

Well suh, right der, Brer Fox set a trap. First, he fetched a rope. Den, he bent down a tree branch a-growin' near de fence-cornder, an tied it ter one end of de rope. On de other end, he make a loop knot, an dat he fasten wid a trigger, right in de hole of de fence. Brer Fox chuckle.

"Dis is de end of Brer Rabbit! Ter-morrer mawnin' I'll have him ketched. Den I'm goin' ter skin him, an I'm goin' ter nail up his hide on de front of my door!" Now Brer Fox go home, an he go ter bed. An all dat night, he dreamed of rabbits, fat rabbits, dancin' round in de moonlight munchin' goobers, an spittin' out de shucks.

Early de next mawnin', while Brer Fox wuz still asleep, sure enuff, along come Brer Rabbit wid a sack slung over his shoulder ter fill up wid goobers. He tiptoe ter de fence, an start ter

30

head. "What sorter wurk is der ter do up der in de air?"

"Skeer-crow sorter wurk. I'm keepin' de crows outer Brer Fox goober patch down der below." Brer Rabbit smile an sway backerds an forerds, hummin' ter hisself. "Brer Fox payin' me lots of money fer dis wurk, Brer Bear."

"Lots of money? How much is he payin' you?"

Now Brer Rabbit take a great big swing, an he crack his heels tergedder, like he de happiest rabbit in dis wurld. "Dollar a minute, Brer Bear!"

"DOLLAR A MINUTE!" Brer Bear just stand der starin' at Brer Rabbit, wid his mouf wide open an his tongue hangin' out.

"Did you ever make a dollar a minute, Brer Bear?"

"No, Brer Rabbit, never!"

"Well . . . wouldn't you like ter make a dollar a minute?"

Brer Bear keep on lookin' at Brer Rabbit danglin' up der in de air on de end of de rope, an he sorter back away. "No, no thankee, Brer Rabbit. I don't know nothin' about dat skeer-crow wurk."

"It's easy wurk, Brer Bear. Der's nothin' to it. All you have ter do is just do nothin', an all de time you're doin' it, de dollars is just pilin' up—big round silver dollars."

"No, no, dem's your silver dollars, Brer Rabbit."

"But I got so many, Brer Bear. My chimbley-cornder is just natchally all stuffed up wid um. Is your chimbley-cornder stuffed up wid big silver dollars, Brer Bear?"

"Oh no, 'tain't stuffed at all."

"Den how you goin' ter buy your fambly der Chrismas presents? Ain't you goin' ter have no turkey? Ain't you goin' ter have mince pie?"

"Well, uh, I ain't thought about dat yet, Brer Rabbit."

"But you oughter think about it. Oh, Brer Bear, you got ter make some money *quick!* I'll have ter give you dis skeer-crow job now—dis very minute!"

"Why, dat's mighty nice of you, Brer Rabbit. You sure is right. I ought ter make some money quick!"

Now Brer Bear can't wait ter get up in de air ter take Brer Rabbit's place. Brer Rabbit show him how ter bend down de tree branch, an it twan't long before Brer Bear wuz swingin' up der on de end of dat rope, an Brer Rabbit wuz sittin' safe an sound on de fence.

Well suh, whiles all dese shinannygins wuz goin' on, Brer Fox wuz just gettin' up outer bed.

He grab up his walkin'-cane, an down he run, *terbuckity-buckity*, straight ter de goober patch. He grin, cause he sure he got Brer Rabbit ketched in de trap. Den all 't once he stop stock still. Der wuz Brer Rabbit, settin' on de fence, gay ez can be.

"Howdy, Brer Fox!" he sing out. "Looks like Brer Bear's been stealin' your goobers. I see you got him ketched here in your trap!"

"Brer Bear!" holler Brer Fox. Now he come a-gallopin'. "Why, dat—dat triflin', good-fer-nothin' slink! Here's wher he gets de wurst lickin' of his life!" Wid dat, he up wid his walkin'-cane an he rush upon Brer Bear.

But Brer Rabbit don't wait ter see de lickin'. He jump down from de fence, he fill up his sack wid ripe, deelicious goobers, an den he skip off home.

How Craney-Crow Kept His Head

DER WUZ one time, I dunno de day, an I dunno de year, but 't wuz one time, when der come a big storm. De wind blowed, an de rain rained like all de sky an de clouds too done turn inter water. De wind blowed so hard dat it lifted a Craney-Crow up from his roost, way down yander in de marshland wher he lived, an it fotched him ter de swampland up here. An when he come, he come a-whirlin'. De wind pick him up an turn him round an round. When it put him down again, he wuz so dizzy, he wobble, like he just learnin' how ter stand up.

By-m-by when de wind stop blowin', he begin ter feel better, an he look round ter find out wher he wuz at. He look an he look but he can't find out, cause ole Craney-Crow wuz a mighty far ways fum home. Yet he wuz standin' in water up ter his knees like he wuz used ter, an dat kinder gave him a cozy home-feelin'. But de swampland here wuz different from de marshland wher he come from. Dis place got thick an tangled grass. An it got vines, an big trees wid moss hangin' down from um like long green whiskers.

Ole Craney-Crow, he feel mighty queer, but he start walkin' round. An when he walk, he look like he's on stilts, his legs wuz so long. De creeturs here, dey holler at him. "Hey! Wher'd you come from? What you doin' here?" Brer Mink an Sis Possum, dey peek round a tree an dey laugh. Brer Mud-Turkle, he bubble up a bubble dat say he laffin' at Craney-Crow, too.

After a while, when de night begin ter drop down, dey let him alone, an den he began pirootin' round ter see what der wuz ter see. Peepin' first in one bush, an den in another, he took notice dat all de birds here in de swampland had gone ter bed widout der heads. Look far ez he can, Craney-Crow can't find one single bird dat hadn't took his head off. Look close ez he can, he can't find one dat had a head on. Craney-Crow ask hisself, "How come dis?" Den he answer hisself, "Goin' ter bed wid der heads on is gone outer fashion in dis part of de country."

Craney-Crow don't know what ter do. He got pride an he don't want ter be outer fashion. He shamed ter go ter bed like he always been doin', an let de other creeturs laff. Yet he don't know how in de name of goodness he goin' ter get his head off. Course he don't know dat de others had just tucked der heads down under der wings. So he look round ter see if der ain't someone he can ask about it. Just den, he see two sharp eyes shinin' at him from somewhers mongst de vines.

"Pardon me, suh," say Craney-Crow, "but I'm a stranger in dese parts, an would you mind tellin' me de reason why all de birds in dis swamp takes der heads off when dey go ter bed?"

De sharp eyes dey squinch up in a sly sorter smile, an out step dat ole rapscallion, Brer Fox. He'd been a-watchin' dis strange bird, an

a-thinkin' how he'd make a mighty pleasant moufful. "Why, stranger," he say, slinkin' up sorter slaunchways, "de reason dey take der heads off is dis. De skeeters here is purty bad, so de birds just natchally get in de habit of takin' der heads off at night, an puttin' um in a safe place."

"But how, suh, does dey do it? It sure stumps me."

"Oh, dey don't do it deyselves," say Brer Fox,

steppin' up real close an lickin' his chops. "Dey got me hired ter do dat fer um."

"An is you hired, suh, ter come back in de mawnin' ter put der heads back on? Cause if you is, suh, I'd like you ter take my head off an put it in a safe place too."

"I'll do dat fer you, stranger. I'll be glad ter."

Wid dat, Brer Fox reach out and grab hold of Craney-Crow's neck, and he start ter squoze it.

Just den, *Pow!* Brer Fox get a whack in de back from someone behind! He fall. Head over tail he splunge inter de water, wid a loud *ker-blashity-blash!* An who should be standin' der, smilin' innocent ez a lamb, but dat smart little Brer Rabbit!

De sleepin' birds, dey hear de racket an dey wake up. Out pop der heads from under der wings. Craney-Crow, he see all de heads an now he understand. He flop his wings, an away he flewed back home. An neither Craney-Crow nor his chilluns, nor even his granchilluns' granchilluns, ain't ever come back ter dis swampland, from dat day down ter dis.

35

Brer Fox, Brer Rabbit, an de Well

ONE DAY in de summertime, Brer Rabbit wuz a-workin' round his front yard. He wuz cuttin' de grass, pullin' up de weeds, an kinder tidyin' things up fer Sunday, when who should come meanderin' along, but ole Brer Fox. He wan't goin' nowhers speshal, an he sorter took a notion ter jump up on de fence an see what Brer Rabbit wuz up ter. Soon ez he seed how hard Brer Rabbit wuz workin' der in de hot sun, he made up his mind dat dis wuz just de time ter have some fun, an make Brer Rabbit mad.

"It's mighty comfortable up here, Brer Rabbit," he sing out, climbin' out on a wide, shady tree-limb. "Course, maybe you likes wurkin' der in de hot sun, but ez fer me, I likes ter stretch out an rest myself in a cool place like dis."

"Well, I like to wurk," say Brer Rabbit. He mop his face wid his hankcher, an begin rakin' up a big mess of leaves. "Some folks in dis neighborhood likes ter lounge round an do nothin', but not Brer Rabbit. I'm a wurkin' man."

Brer Fox yawn. "Dat's mighty lucky, Brer Rabbit, cause you sure got plenty of wurk ter do, an you ain't goin' have no time ter stretch out an rest yourself in a cool place like dis."

Now Brer Rabbit wuz gettin' tired, an restin' hisself in a cool place like dat wuz exactly what he had in mind. Howsomever, he don't want Brer Fox ter go blabbin' round dat he's lazy.

So . . . he just keep on rakin' fer a while. But after a bit, he kinder smile ter hisself, an he say kinder loud, "Now I got ter take dese leaves around ter de trash pile behind de house an burn um." Wid dat, he scoop up a big armful of leaves, an trot off. But he don't take um ter de trash pile. He dump um just round de house-cornder. Den he look round fer a cool place ter rest hisself—a place where Brer Fox can't see him.

All 't once, he happen ter glance at de old stone well. "Just de place!" he say. He look down inside, an der at de bottom, on de end of a rope, wuz a bucket, just settin' down der on top of de water. He look up at de roof of de well, an der wuz another bucket, danglin' from de other end of de rope, an swingin' in de air.

Brer Rabbit grin. "Dis bucket up here is just de place ter rest myself. An Brer Fox'll never find me. Dat's sure." Wid dat, he jump in. But he ain't no sooner got inside, dan dis bucket begun ter go down, an de other bucket begun ter go up! Down go Brer Rabbit, down, down, till his bucket hit de water—*kersplash,* an de empty bucket hit de roof—*kerblip!* Brer Rabbit's bucket float der on de water. Brer Rabbit, he skeered most outer his skin. All he can see is de dark insides of de well. All he can hear is de water a-swishin' an a-swashin' all around him. An der ain't no way ter get out.

Now of course all dis while, Brer Fox wan't doin' any nappin'. He always got one eye on Brer Rabbit, an when he seed him sneak off, round de cornder of de house, he sneak along right behind. He seed Brer Rabbit go ter de well. He seed him jump inter de bucket. An he seed de bucket wid Brer Rabbit in it go down outer sight.

Brer Fox can't skacely believe his eyes. He puzzle an puzzle but he can't make head nor tails outer dat kinder goin's-on. He creep along on his tippy-toes close ter de well, an he lissen, but he don't hear nothin'. Den he creep up still closer. He peep down, but he don't see nothin'. Natchally, der wuzzent nothin' ter see, cause Brer Rabbit wuz just sottin' der in de dark, so skeered he dasn't even move his eye-balls.

By-m-by, Brer Fox lean way over de edge of de well, an he holler down, "Heyo, Brer Rabbit! What in de dickens is you doin' down der?"

"Shhhh!" holler up Brer Rabbit. "Dat's a secret."

"Well . . . er . . . is de water very wet down der, Brer Rabbit?"

"Oh, not so wet ez it might be on a rainy day, Brer Fox. But dat don't make much difference anyhow, cause I'm havin' such a lot of fun down here."

"Fun?" Now Brer Fox lean way, way over de

edge an stare down inter de darkness. "What sorter fun at de bottom of a deep, dark well?"

Brer Rabbit chuckle. "Ain't you never heard tell about de fitsy-fotsy-figgaloo fishes? Ain't you never heard tell dat dese fishes don't live nowher else exceptin' just down here?"

Now Brer Rabbit talkin' so nice an chummy, dat Brer Fox don't suspicion nothin'. "Why, I ain't never heard nothin' about um, Brer Rabbit. What sorter fishes is fitsy-fotsy-figgaloo fishes?"

"Why, dey's de most expensive fishes in de wurld, Brer Fox. I ketch um here, an den I take um ter town on Fridays, an I sells um ter de rich folks fer $50 a pound!"

"Um! $50 a pound!" Brer Fox gasp. "Well . . . er . . . is der many of dose fitsy-fotsy-figgaloo fishes down der?"

"Lots of um, Brer Fox, scoze an scoze of um! De water is just natchally alive wid um!"

"Well den, Brer Rabbit, don't you need someone ter kinder help you haul um in?"

Brer Rabbit don't answer fer a minute, like he sorter mullin' dis matter over in his mind. "Maybe I do need a helper. Dat's a good idea, Brer Fox."

Now Brer Fox so anxious ter get some of dose fishes fer hisself, his heart wuz poundin' like a hammer. "But how am I goin' ter get down der ter help you, Brer Rabbit?"

"Why, dat's easy, Brer Fox. Just jump inter dat empty bucket up der. It'll fetch you down here in a jiffy."

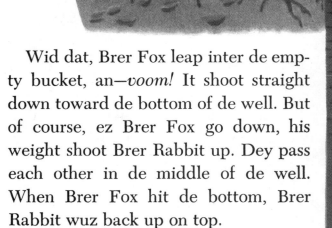

Wid dat, Brer Fox leap inter de empty bucket, an—*voom!* It shoot straight down toward de bottom of de well. But of course, ez Brer Fox go down, his weight shoot Brer Rabbit up. Dey pass each other in de middle of de well. When Brer Fox hit de bottom, Brer Rabbit wuz back up on top.

Brer Rabbit hop out. Den he lean over de edge, an he holler down inter de dark, "Haul in ez many of dose fitsy-fotsy-figgaloo fish ez you can, Brer Fox! Den just stretch out an rest yourself in dat nice, cool place down der."

Wid dat, Brer Rabbit prance right back ter wurk again, cause now dat he got rid of dat busy-body Fox; he don't feel tired any more.

Brer Rabbit's Money Machine

ONE MAWNIN', Brer Rabbit had been off ter town a-sellin' watermellions, an his pockets wuz just crammed full wid money. On de road goin' home, it just so happened dat he met up wid Brer Bear.

"Howdy, Brer Bear!" he sing out. He feel so gay dat he prance right up an shake hands. "How's Mrs. Bear? How's your two chilluns, Kubs an Klibs?"

"Dey's purty well, Brer Rabbit. How's Mrs. Rabbit an your forty-seven little Rabbit chilluns?"

"Fine, fine—all fine!" Now Brer Rabbit feel just in de mood fer cuttin' up, an he notice dat Brer Bear look like he sorter dopey, an not really awake from his head all de way down ter his tail.

Well, Brer Rabbit begin dancin' round, an of course, de money in his pocket begin ter jingle.

Brer Bear cock up his ears. "Huh? If I ain't

mighty much mistaken, Brer Rabbit, I hear de jinglin' of money."

Brer Rabbit sorter grin an hold his head keerless. " 'T ain't nothin' much—just a bit of small change." Wid dat, he reached in his pocket, an drawed out a whole pawful of silver quarters, all shiny an spankin' brand new.

Brer Bear's big mouf drop open wide. "Laws a massy, Brer Rabbit! Wh— wh— wher in de name of goodness did you get all dat money?"

Brer Rabbit put de money back in his pocket, an he answer kinder slow. "Oh, I gets it wher dey make it. I always gets it der."

"Wher dey make it?" Brer Bear so 'stonished his tongue get all tangled up in his mouf. "Wwwww—wwww—llll—lll, well, wherbouts is it dey—dey make dat money?"

Brer Rabbit roll his eyes round, an den he whisper, like he don't want no one else ter hear, "Why, sometimes dey makes it in one place, an other times, dey makes it in another. You got ter do like me, Brer Bear, an keep your eyes watchin' sharp."

"Yes, yes, I'll keep my eyes watchin' sharp! But tell me, please tell me, Brer Rabbit, how I can find dat money-place too!"

He beg an he beg, but Brer Rabbit just kinder study him, like he got some doubts on his mind. Den he sot down on a rock, Brer Rabbit did, an he just fool round in de sand wid his foot. Bym-by he say, "Spozen I do tell you de place. How do I know you ain't goin' ter blab it round de whole neighborhood? Den everybody'll go grabblin' fer de money, an we won't get none at all."

Brer Bear, he vow an swear an cross his heart dat he won't tell one livin' breathin' soul. He so excited he begin ter trimble an shake.

Now Brer Rabbit sidle up real close ter Brer Bear like he tellin' him de most secret secret in de wurld. " 'T ain't such a hard place ter find, once you know how. All you got ter do is ter watch de road till you see a waggin come along. Den, if you look real close, you'll see dat de waggin—if it's de right kinder waggin—has got two front wheels an two behind wheels. Fuddermore, you'll see dat de front wheels is lots littler dan de behind wheels. Now, when you see dat, what does your common sense tell you goin' ter happen?"

"Well—er—well," Brer Bear scratch his head. "Dat's too much fer me, Brer Rabbit."

Brer Rabbit pull down de cornders of his mouf, sorter disgusted, like he never met up wid such a numbskull ez Brer Bear. "Your common sense oughter tell you dat purty soon de big behind wheels goin' ter ketch up wid de little front wheels."

"Sure enuff," say Brer Bear, "dat must be so."

"Now," say Brer Rabbit, "if you know dat de big wheels goin' ter ketch de little wheels, an dat every time dey grind up gainst one another, shiny, brand-new money goin' ter drop from betwixt um . . . well . . . what your common sense tell you ter do den?"

"Why . . . er. . . ." Brer Bear hang his head like his common sense don't tell him ter noth-in' at all.

Now Brer Rabbit act like he losin' patience wid de common sense Brer Bear ain't got. "Dis is what you do," he say, sorter cross. "If you don't want no brand new money, you can just sit down an let de waggin go on by. But if you do want de money, you can foller along an keep

watch. Den, when de behind wheels get ter grindin' against de front ones, an de money starts ter drop down, you'll be right der ter ketch it."

Brer Rabbit jump up. "Lissen, Brer Bear. . . . I hear a waggin comin' now!"

Sure enuff, just den, a waggin come rumblin' down de road.

Brer Rabbit, he slap Brer Bear on de back. "What luck! It's de right kinder waggin, wid de big wheels in back, an de little ones in front! Here's your chance, Brer Bear!"

Now Brer Bear wuz starin' at de waggin wid his eyes shinin' like stars, an he wuz shakin' all over. Up he scramble, an away he race, puffin' an pantin' along right beside de waggin.

"Watch dose wheels, Brer Bear! Watch um close!" holler out Brer Rabbit. "An I'll drop by an tell Mrs. Bear ter go buy herself a fine, han-some present, cause you're goin' ter be oh, *so rich!*"

But soon ez Brer Bear wuz outer sight, Brer Rabbit just lay down in de grass, ter kick up his heels an haw-haw.

Brer Rabbit an de Huckleberry Jam

DER WUZ one time, way back, when times wuz hard. De creeturs had ter grub round fer vittles ter eat, an sometimes dey most had ter scratch gravel ter get enuff. Dey ain't had time fer foolin' each other an playing tricks; dey had ter hire deyselves out wheresomever der wuz wurk.

De first week er two, Brer Rabbit wurk purty hard. He pick cotton, he split up kindlin' wood, he rake up leaves, an he wuz much too tired ter cut up capers at all. Den come de day—when he an Brer Fox wuz bof hired tergedder—ter patch up a leak in de roof of a barn.

When Brer Rabbit hear dat Brer Fox an he got ter wurk on de same job, he feel kinder dubious. "I don't like joinin' up wid dat snaggle-toofed, bushy-tail trash," he say ter Mrs. Rabbit.

"Never you mind," say Mrs. Rabbit. "Just you keep bof eyes open and bof ears hoist up . . . now run along." Wid dat, she pack him up a little lunch ter take wid him, ter eat when de job wuz done.

Brer Rabbit grumble a bit, but he take de lunch, an he start off. On de way, he meet Brer Fox, an he wuz carryin a box of lunch too. "Howdy!" say Brer Rabbit, actin' sorter sociable. "De sun's shinin' mighty hot terday. I expect we better leave dese lunches down by de spring wher dey'll keep cool."

"Sure enuff," say Brer Fox. "Dat's just what we'll do."

Now whiles dey wuz puttin' der lunches

43

down der by de spring, Brer Rabbit just happen ter notice dat Brer Fox lunch wuz fixed up mighty tasty, wid a big jar of huckleberry jam fer dessert. But he don't say nothin', an he an Brer Fox go along ter de barn wher dey goin' ter fix de roof.

Well suh, dey climbed up, an dey went ter wurk. Brer Rabbit, he stuck a pencil behind his ear, an went round measurin' an markin' wher de new roof shingles wuz ter go. Brer Fox, he pick up de hammer, some nails an de new shingles, an start fastenin' um on.

Dey wurk an dey wurk, but 'twan't long before Brer Rabbit feel a sorter honger in his innerds, an his stummock begin ter growl. 'Tain't been but a while since he had brekfus, but he feel like he can eat a hoss. He can't keep his mind off Brer Fox jar of huckleberry jam, lyin' down der by de spring. "I just got ter have some," he say ter hisself, "just a teenchy little taste."

First thing you know, whilst Brer Fox wuz kickin' up a racket wid de hammer, Brer Rabbit jump down from de roof an hop off. He scoot down ter de spring, an grab hisself a big lick of dat jam straight outer de jar. Den he go a-scallyootin' back, an climb up on de roof again.

"Wher you been?" ask Brer Fox.

"Dis hot sun make me dizzy in de head," say Brer Rabbit, moppin' his face wid his hankcher. "I just had ter go rest myself fer a minute in de shade."

"Hmmmph!" snort Brer Fox, like he suspicioned somethin'.

Brer Rabbit wurk on a while, but de teenchy little taste of dat huckleberry jam wuz just enuff ter make his mouf begin ter water fer some more. He wait till he seed Brer Fox go crawlin' round de roof-cornder. Den down he go again ter de spring. Now dat jam taste even more deelicious dan before. He stay a while, an he gobble up half de jar.

Brer Fox wuz waitin' fer him when he got back dis time, an his eyes looked mighty sharp. "Wher you been now? You been gone a long time."

"One of dese flyin' bugs up here done bit me way down inside my ear. I had ter run home an get de soothin' salve." Brer Rabbit scratch his ear wid his behind foot like it hurt him. "Dese bugs is red waspies, an der sting sure is turrible bad."

Brer Fox frown like he don't exactly believe dis story, but anyhow, dey bof go back ter wurk. But Brer Rabbit can't think of nothin' but

how he goin' ter get dose last licks of huckle-berry jam, just goin' ter waste der in de jar. Presently, he cock up his ears, like he hear some noise way far off. "Laws-a-massy!" he yell. "It's Mrs. Rabbit callin'! Somethin' turrible must be de matter at home! I got ter run find out what 'tis!"

Wid dat he jump down from de roof an away he scoot, straight back ter de spring again. Now he guzzle up all Brer Fox huckleberry jam, right down ter de bottom of de jar. He lick it dry. Den he hurry up back ter wurk.

Brer Fox wuz waitin' fer him, pacin' up an down de roof, a-switchin' his tail. "Well, what wuz de matter at home?"

Brer Rabbit pant, like he been runnin' far. "Oh, de neighbor's chilluns come by an flung a rock at one of my chilluns, an hit her on de top of de head where de cow-lick is. . . . I had ter run fer de doctor!"

Brer Fox, he slam down his hammer—*ker-blam!* "I'm sick an tired of wurkin' here in de sun whiles you keep runnin' off. I done had ter finish up dis whole job alone, an I'm goin' see to it dat you don't get one cent of pay. But furst, I'm goin' down ter de spring ter eat my lunch. I'm hungry!"

"Me too," say Brer Rabbit, kinder winkin' his eye. "I'm monstus hongry."

Wid dat, dey bof jump down from de roof an start fer de spring, but Brer Rabbit, bein' de fastest, gets der furst. He paw up de earf, an scuff up a few pebbles, like somebody already been der, snoozlin' round. Den he sing out, "Quick! Quick, Brer Fox! Looks like somebody's been here! Oh gracious! Oh goodness! Some-body *has* been here! Somebody's eat up all your huckleberry jam!" Brer Rabbit open his eyes up very wide, an he stand der starin' at de empty jar.

Brer Fox come trottin' up. He see de empty jar. He growl. Den his eye just happen ter glance up at Brer Rabbit. Der, stuck ter de tip-end of his mustarsh, wuz a little round drop of huckle-berry jam! Brer Fox let out a squall dat mighter been heard forty mile. "Why, you . . . you . . . you worfless, weazly *wump!*" Wid dat he make a snatch fer Brer Rabbit, but he just lack a little bit of bein' quick enuff.

Brer Rabbit, he grab up his lunch; he take a big leap, an off he race like his tail wuz afire. Brer Fox, he race right after him. Dey race an dey race, till purty soon, Brer Rabbit lead dat Fox ter de brier-patch. He zigzag in an out mongst de briers. But Brer Fox ain't made fer

dat scratchy sorter bizness. He get scraggled up in de pricklers an he can't get nowhers. He just get madder an madder an madder till he well-nigh plum crazy.

Den Brer Rabbit zip away. Soon ez he wuz outer smellin' distance, he skip back ter de barn, an get his pay. Now, wid de huckleberry jam in his stummock, wid his lunch under his arm, wid a heap of money jinglin' in his pocket . . . an wid Brer Fox thrashin' round up yander in de brier-patch . . . Brer Rabbit wuz ez happy ez can be.

De Wuller-de-Wust

"'M TIRED of eatin' cabbiges," say Brer Rabbit one mawnin'. "An I'm tired of carrots, sparrer-grass an beans. I'd like ter sink my teef in somethin' sweet." Wid dat, he took a notion ter run over ter Brer Bear's house, ter see what dey had ter eat over der.

Whiles he wuz lippity-clippitin' along on his way, lo an behold, who should he meet up wid but Brer Bear hisself. Mrs. Bear wuz strollin' beside him, and shufflin' along right behind wuz der two chilluns, Kubs an Klibs.

"Howdy!" say Brer Rabbit, makin' a bow real perlite.

"Howdy!" say Brer Bear and Mrs. Bear, bowin' just ez perlite. Den Kubs an Klibs, dey say Howdy, an dey bow too.

Brer Rabbit, he sot down on his hunkers till dey pass by. "Hmmm," he think. "Dat Bear fambly is round an fat ez a dish of butter balls. Dey must have somethin' sweet an tasty in der pantry cubbud, an I'm goin' have a lick of it right now."

Now Brer Rabbit take a short cut throo de bushes, an he get ter Brer Bear's house while der ain't nobody der. He walk in de front door an begin a-sniffin' an a-snuffin' round. He peep in here; he poke in der. He nibble a little of dis;

47

he gobble a little of dat. Den all 't once, he spy a bucket of honey, way on a high-up shelf. "Mmmm . . . mmmm!" Brer Rabbit smack his lips. He start scramblin' up, an he make a grab fer dat honey-bucket, when—*pow!* it come tumblin' down. It slosh all over him; just a little more an he'd been drowned. From de top of his ears ter de tip of his tail, he wuz just drippin' wid gooey, gluey honey.

Brer Rabbit lick up a big moufful, an den he ask hisself, "What'll I do now? If I stay in here, Brer Bear'll come back an ketch me. But I'm ashamed ter go outside anywhers, an let de other creeturs see me all stuck-up like dis. Fer massy sake, what *will* I do?"

Well, by-m-by, Brer Rabbit open de door an sneak out. Now of course, de honey make his foots sorter slippery, an de furst thing you know, right der in Brer Bear's front yard, he fall down. He roll over in de leaves. De leaves, dey stick. He kick an scuff dis way an dat ter knock um off, but de more he scuff, de more dey stick. 'Twan't long before he wuz kivvered all over wid leaves. Den he stand up an try ter shake um off, but dey still stick. An wid every shake he make, de leaves, dey go *swishy-swushy, splishy-splushy.* By dis time, Brer Rabbit wuz de skeeriest-lookin', and de skeeriest-soundin', creetur you ever laid your eyes on.

Whiles he wuz standin' der, figgerin' out what ter do next, who should happen ter come saunterin' by, but ole Sis Cow. No sooner did she ketch sight of Brer Rabbit in dose leaves dan she set up a howl, an off she gallop, a-mooin' an a-booin' like she seed a ghost.

Brer Rabbit laff.

Now who should come floppin' down outer de air, but Brer Tukkey Buzzard! He take just one look at Brer Rabbit. Den he flip his wings, an he yank hisself right up inter de air again, screechin' an squallin' till he wuz way up outer sight somewhers in de clouds.

Dis make Brer Rabbit laff some more. He begin ter be mighty pleased about bein' such a skeery-lookin' creetur, an he feel like cuttin' up. Just den, he see Brer Fox come struttin' along, swingin' his fancy walkin'-cane. Brer Rabbit chuckle. He jump out inter de middle of de road, an he give hisself a great big shake . . . *swishy-swushy, splishy-splushy.* Den he kinder sing-song, low an mysterious:

> "I'm de Wuller-de-Wust
> An You're de One I'm after.
> I think I'll skin you just fer fun—
>> You better run,
>> You better run,
> Cause I'm de Wuller-de-Wust
> An You're de One I'm after."

Well suh, run wuz just what dat Fox done do. He drop his fancy walkin'-cane an he race off inter de woods. "Oh! Oh, Lawdy! Oh!" he yell, leapin' straight throo de bushes.

Now Brer Rabbit feel so sassy he want ter skeer everybody in de neighborhood. "I'll just wait here an skeer de Bear fambly when dey get back from der walk," he chuckle ter hisself. "I'll skeer um all . . . de whole caboodle." Wid dat, he sot down ter wait in de shade of de tree by Brer Bear's front porch. Purty soon, he got ter feelin' sorter drowsy, an de next thing you know, he dozed off.

Whiles he wuz a-dozin' der in de shade, de

sun moved round a bit, till by-m-by, Brer Rabbit wuzn't dozin' in de shade no more. He wuz dozin' right in de sizzlin' sun. De sun, it dry up de honey dat wuz kivverin' Brer Rabbit. An de leaves dat wuz stickin' ter de honey dropped off. Now Brer Rabbit don't look like a skeery-creetur no more; he look just like hisself. But of course, bein' asleep, Brer Rabbit don't know dis.

De furst thing he know, he hear de trompin' of big, heavy foots. Der wuz de Bear fambly, comin' right up toward de porch. Brer Rabbit jump up quick. He leap out from under de tree, an start ter moan:

> "*I'm de Wuller-de-Wust*
>   *An You're de Ones I'm after.*
> *I think I'll skin you just fer fun—*
>   *You better run,*
>   *You better run,*
> *Cause I'm de Wuller-de-Wust*
>   *An You're de Ones I'm after.*"

De Bear fambly dey stare at Brer Rabbit wid der moufs open wide. Den Brer Bear, he bust out laffin'. "Wuller-de-Wust? What in de name of goodness is de matter wid you, Brer Rabbit? An what's dat dried-up stuff all over you? You're de frowsiest-lookin' creetur I ever did see!"

Brer Rabbit, he look down, an he see dat de leaves dat wuz kivverin' him wuz all gone. An just at dat minute, Brer Bear, he see dat his front door wuz wide open, an dat Brer Rabbit's sticky footprints wuz on de porch.

Brer Bear growl. "Why, you—you—you been messin' round in my honey, you scoundul!" Brer Bear, he reach out an make a grab fer Brer Rabbit. But Brer Bear ain't made ter move very fast, an Brer Rabbit wuz already scootin' outer der, faster dan a streak of lightnin'.

He scooted way off, ter de edge of de river. Den he squot down, an he look at hisself in de water. "Well," he say, "maybe I ain't de skeeriest creetur on dis earf, but I'm de smartest, an de fastest, an I surely have de most fun." Wid dat, he start washin' off de dried-up honey in de clear, cool water, till purty soon, he wuz all slicked up, like brand new.

De Moon in de Mill-Pond

ER WUZ one night when Brer Rabbit an Brer Terrapin wuz just sittin' off in de woods, talkin' about ole times. De woods wuz cold, but dey had a big warm fire. De woods wuz dark, but up in de sky wuz a big shinin' moon. De woods wuz quiet, but Brer Rabbit had his big banjo.

"Come on, Brer Rabbit," say Brer Terrapin, stretchin' his neck out closer ter de fire. "Let's have a tune."

Brer Rabbit sot down on his hunkers an began ter tune up. "Plank . . . plink . . . plink . . . plank." . . . But just den, he hear a kinder stirrin' in de bushes right close by. He cock up his ears an lissen. "Who's der?"

"'T ain't nobody," say Brer Terrapin . . . "It's only de fireflies lightin' up der fires."

"Hush up!" Brer Rabbit cock his ears up higher, an lissen some more.

"Maybe it's de night owl shakin' de day off his fedders."

"Shhhhhh . . . it's Brer Fox an Brer Bear!" Now Brer Rabbit sniff trubble. "Sure ez you live, dey're plannin' how ter nab us, an roast us fer der dinner, right here on dis fire."

Well suh, Brer Rabbit, he begin plannin' too. First, he begin bustlin' round de fire. He poke at de ashes. He heave on a big chunk of wood. Den he wink at Brer Terrapin, an he say sorter loud, . . . "Dis fire got ter be just hot enuff—but not too hot—cause we got a real feast ter cook ter-night." He smack his lips. "Say, Brer Terrapin . . . how we goin' ter eat such a smashin' big dinner all alone? What a pity we ain't got no company!"

Now de stirrin' in de bushes get real noisy, an out tromp Brer Fox an Brer Bear, lookin' just ez innocent ez a pair of chipmonks.

"Bless my soul if it ain't Brer Fox an Brer Bear!" sing out Brer Rabbit, prancin' up an shakin' hands. "Come over ter de fire an warm yourselves . . . we're surely glad ter see you! Why, just dis very minute Brer Terrapin an me wuz wonderin' how we wuz goin' ter eat such a smashin' big dinner all alone."

Brer Fox an Brer Bear, dey sorta snuff round.

"I don't see no smashin' big dinner," say Brer Fox.

"Nor me," say Brer Bear. He lick out his tongue like he gettin' hongry.

Brer Terrapin, he pull his head back inside his shell, cause he mighty skeered. But Brer Rabbit just keep on actin' like everything wuz fine.

"Course you don't see de dinner now . . . but just you wait." Brer Rabbit fuss round in de ashes some more like he fixin' up a place ter put a great big pot.

"But . . . where is dis smashin' big dinner?" Brer Fox squint up his eyes like he begin ter suspicion somethin'.

"Right down at de mill-pond," whisper Brer

Rabbit. "Shhh!" He roll his eyes round toward de bushes like he afraid someone'll hear. "It's waitin' der dis very minute! . . . de finest mess of fishes in all dis wurld!"

"What kinder fishes?" ask Brer Bear, sidlin' up closer an closer ter Brer Terrapin, like he got a better idea dan fishes.

"De fattest, juiciest, most deelicious fishes you ever laid your eyes on! . . . Mmmm . . . Mm-mmm!" say Brer Rabbit, lickin' his chops.

"Hmmph!" snort Brer Fox. "How you goin' ter ketch um? I don't see no fish-line, an I don't see no pole." Now he slink right up beside Brer Rabbit, an rub his hot nose on Brer Rabbit's ear.

Brer Rabbit don't like dis, but he keep on actin' like everything wuz fine. "Why, ketchin' um's easy . . . shhhh!" Now he whisper like he don't want even de gnats an de beetles ter hear de secret. "Dese fishes ain't no ordinary sorter fishes! On a night like dis, when de moon's up der in de sky, dese fishes come right up ter de top of de water, an dey dance . . . *hippity flippity!* All you have ter do is reach down wid your paw, an scoop um up! Come on, everybody! It's gettin' late, an I'm gettin' hongry!"

Brer Fox an Brer Bear, dey wink at each other. Now dey think dey may ez well get der share of dese deelicious fishes. Den dey can roast up Brer Rabbit an Brer Terrapin fer dessert.

Well suh, dey all march down ter de pond. Brer Rabbit, he feel de cold chills racin' up his back, cause he know der ain't goin' ter be no deelicious fishes, dancin' *hippity flippity* on de top of de water. He have ter wurk his mind purty fast. But he skip along real frisky, just like everything wuz fine.

Now of course, bein' de fastest, Brer Rabbit gets ter de pond furst, an when he looks down inter de water, what's he see but de moon! Der it wuz, shinin' down from de sky, but lookin' like it wuz layin' der at de very bottom of de pond. Brer Rabbit chuckle ter hisself, cause now he know what he goin' ter do!

By dis time, Brer Fox, Brer Bear an Brer Terrapin were comin' up close. Brer Rabbit lean out over de edge of de pond, an stare down. "Oh dear! . . . oh my! . . . tch . . . tch . . . tch!" he cry, like he see something turrible bad.

"What in de wurld is de matter, Brer Rabbit?" holler Brer Fox an Brer Bear bofe at once. Brer Terrapin don't say nothin', cause he don't know exactly what Brer Rabbit plannin' ter do.

Brer Rabbit just keep on starin' down inter de pond. Now de others wuz starin' down too, searchin' fer de dancin' fishes.

Brer Rabbit sigh. "Bad . . . mighty bad! But accidents got ter happen sometimes, an dis is just one of dose accidents. De moon done drop down inter de pond an skeered all de dancin' fishes away! Look way, *way* down, an you'll see it down der fer yourselves."

Dey look, an sure enuff, der lay de moon, a-swingin' an a-swayin' at de very bottom of de pond. Brer Fox grumble. Brer Bear growl.

"Gentermens," say Brer Rabbit, "you can grumble an growl ez much ez you please, but unless we get dat moon outer dis pond, we ain't goin' ter have no fish dinner ter-night."

"An just how are we goin' ter get dat moon outer dis pond?" ask Brer Fox, actin' mighty snarly.

"How?" say Brer Rabbit. "Well . . . I expect de best way is fer me ter run round ter ole Mr. Mud Turkle an ask him ter loan us his fishin' net. Wid dat, we'll drag de moon out from under de water in no time at all."

Well . . . Brer Rabbit, he ran fer de net. But Brer Fox an Brer Bear, dey wuz gettin' hongrier an hongrier. Dey kinder squint der eyes at little Brer Terrapin, an dey smack der lips.

Now Brer Terrapin powerful skeered, but his mind wuz wurkin' powerful fast. He stick his head outer his shell, an he whisper, "Pssst . . . psstt!" like he got a secret ter tell whiles Brer

Rabbit wuz runnin' ter get de net. Brer Fox an Brer Bear, dey come up close.

Brer Terrapin whisper some more. "More strange doin's goes on round dis mill-pond dan most folks know. But I know, an de lizzuds know . . . an de bull-frogs . . . we know about dat pot of gold."

"*What* pot of gold?" ask Brer Fox an Brer Bear bofe tergedder.

"Dat pot of gold down on de bottom of de pond right wher de moon is . . . shhhhhhhh . . . here come Brer Rabbit . . . don't say a wurd!"

Up prance Brer Rabbit, *lippity clippity*, draggin' de big net behind him. He wink at Brer Terrapin, cause he understand why he wuz a-whisperin' like dat.

"Now fer dat moon!" sing out Brer Rabbit. He fling off his coat. He rip off his pants, like he can't

55

get inter dat pond fast enuff. Den Brer Fox an Brer Bear, dey fling off der coats. Dey rip off der pants, like dey can't get inter dat pond fast enuff. Dey snatch de net away from Brer Rabbit, an dey push him back.

Splish! Splosh! Brer Fox an Brer Bear jump down from de bank inter de low water. Dey wade out. Dey spread out de big net. Dey drag it back an forth throo de water . . . but dey don't haul in de moon, an dey don't haul in de gold.

Dey spread it an drag it some more. Again . . . no moon, no gold!

Dey wade out furder an spread it an drag it. Still again, no moon, no gold!

Brer Rabbit an Brer Terrapin, dey watch from de bank an just grin. "Go on still furder!" dey holler. "You ain't gone far enuff!"

Well suh, dey go on still furder, till all 't once . . . *kerplunk!* Down dey step inter a great deep hole, an fall in. "Help! Help!" dey yelp, gulpin' in big mouffuls of de muddy pond water. Dey howl; dey yowl. Dey kick an thrash, an dey get all tangled up in de fish net. An de more dey kick an thrash, de more tangled up dey get.

Back on de dry land, Brer Rabbit an Brer Terrapin don't wait ter help um ontangle der entanglement. Dey skip off throo de woods, laffin' an laffin' till it hurt um ter laff, an dey 'fraid der sides wuz goin' ter crack open. Den dey laff just once more, fer good measure.

Brer Rabbit Goes a-Milkin'

ONE DAY, Brer Rabbit wuz prancin' long de road *lippity clippity*, like he always do, but he wuz feelin' sorter tired an stiff in his joints, an his tongue wuz hangin' outer his mouf fer want of somethin' ter drink. By-m-by, he seed ole Sis Cow grazin' round in a field just over de fence.

Brer Rabbit, he study her fer a minute, an he begin ter wurk his mind. Purty soon, he get an idea, cause he too smart ter go round feelin' thirsty very long.

Well . . . he sorter dance up long side de fence, an he bow real perlite. "Howdy, Sis Cow!"

Sis Cow look up. She bow real perlite too. "Howdy, Brer Rabbit! Howdy do!"

"How you feelin' dese days, Sis Cow? An how's Brer Bull?"

"Oh . . . we're sorter so-so, thank you, Brer Rabbit. How you feelin' yourself?"

"Oh . . . I'm sorter so-so too, thank you." Den Brer Rabbit roll his eyes around, an he glance up at a tree close by. "Say . . . Sis Cow . . . just take a look at dose nice crab apples a-growin' on dat

tree. Mmmmmm . . . Mmmmm! I'd sure like ter have some of um!"

"How you goin' ter get um, Brer Rabbit? Dey're up der purty high."

"Well, I wuz just thinkin' dat maybe you'd be kind enuff ter knock against de tree trunk wid one of your horns, an shake de crab apples down."

"Why, I'd be glad ter do dat fer you, Brer Rabbit, seein' ez how you ain't got no horns yourself." Wid dat, Sis Cow march up ter de crab apple tree an hit it a rap wid one of her horns. *Blip!*

Now dose crab apples wuz green, an not ready ter come off, so not one single one of um drop down. Sis Cow, she try again. Dis time, she sorter back off a little, an run up against de tree wid bofe her horns. *Blap!* Still no crab apples drop down. Sis Cow, she frown. Den she back way off. She hoist up her tail an she come gallopin' straight inter dat tree . . . *kerblam!* She come so fast an so hard, dat her horns plunk right inter de tree an stick der. Der she wuz . . . stuck! She can't go forerds an she can't go backerds.

57

"Help! Help!" she yell, twistin' an pullin' an kickin' up de earf. "Get me outer here!"

Of course dis wuz exactly what Brer Rabbit wuz waitin' fer. Way down in his stummock he laugh, but he don't let on. "Oh dear! Oh my! Gracious goodness!" he cry. "Sis Cow, I'm afraid I ain't strong enuff ter pull you outer der. Dis is a job fer Brer Bull! I'll run an fetch him quick!"

Wid dat, Brer Rabbit skip off. But he don't fetch Brer Bull. He fetch Mrs. Rabbit, Miss Rabbit, Junior Rabbit an all de little Rabbits too. An when dey prance up alongside ole Sis Cow, every last one of um wuz carryin' a pail! De big ones had big pails, an de little ones had little pails. Dey all gathered round Sis Cow an began ter milk her.

Sis Cow, she kick an she stomp. She switch her tail an try ter knock over de pails, but der wuz enuff rabbits in de Rabbit fambly ter hold um down. Dey milked an dey milked till de pails wuz all full. Den dey just went scamperin' home, an Brer Rabbit had plenty of milk fer hisself an all de fambly fer a long, long time.

Brer Possum
Plays Possum

ONE AFTERNOON, Brer Coon an Brer Possum wuz amblin' along throo de woods, just havin' some fun. Now an den, dey'd pass by a persimmons tree. Den, Brer Coon would have ter wait while Brer Possum climb up. He'd crawl out ter de end of a branch, an hang der by his tail, stuffin' his mouf wid persimmons till he couldn't hold no more. Den, down he'd come, an dey'd amble along some more, till dey'd pass by a brook. Now 'twuz Brer Possum's turn ter wait, while Brer Coon reach in de water an ketch hisself a pawful of frogs. Dey meandered along dis way just ez chummy ez you please, till by-m-by dey seed Brer Fox a-slinkin' round.

Now Brer Coon smelt trubble. He step up close ter Brer Possum an he whisper, "Dat Fox is hidin' der wher de bushes is thick an de shadders black. He's fixin' up ter make a splunge at us, sure ez I'm Coon."

59

"Shucks! don't you worry," say Brer Possum. "You just let me take care of him." Brer Possum arch up his back an hoist up his tail, like he feel strong enuff ter lick a hundred Brer Foxes.

Well suh, de very next minute dat Fox come a-zoomin'! He sail right inter Brer Possum an he ketch him square in de ribs. Brer Possum, he let out a squeal an boo-hoo. Den he just keel over, an he lay der like he wuz dead.

Now Brer Fox sail inter Brer Coon. He snatch at him wid toof an claw. Brer Coon snatch back. Den he reach out an give dat Fox a biff dat sent him sprawlin'. When Brer Fox got back enuff bref ter scramble up again, he had ter count his-self ter see if he all der. Den, what wuz left of him went limpin' off throo de woods.

Now Brer Coon look down at Brer Possum, playin' dead der in de dust. He don't care fer cowards, an he turn up his nose. He brush de hunks of fox fur off his coat, an off he go on his way.

Next day, Brer Possum meet Brer Coon down at de creek. "Howdy!" he sing out.

Brer Coon don't answer. He turn his back.

Dis make Brer Possum feel mighty bad, seein' ez how dey wuz so chummy de afternoon before. "What's de matter wid you, Brer Coon? Ain't we friends?"

Brer Coon hold his chin up high, an he say, "I ain't got no time ter waste wid cowards. Leave me alone."

Now Brer Possum sorter mad. "Who's a coward?" he say.

"You is," say Brer Coon. "Dat's who. I ain't associatin' wid skeer-cats dat lays down an plays dead when der's a free fight goin' on."

Brer Possum laff. "Lawsy sakes! Did you think I wuz layin' down cause I wuz skeered? Why, I wuzn't skeered at all! I wuz just layin' der ad-mirin' de way you wuz moppin' up de earf wid Brer Fox, an waitin' my turn ter do dat very thing too!"

"Is dat so? Hmmpf!" snort Brer Coon. "Why, de very first minute Brer Fox smash inter you, I seed you boo-hoo an keel over like you wuz dead."

Brer Possum laff again. "Why, I wuzn't boo-hoo cryin'; I wuz boo-hoo laffin'! When Brer Fox stuck his nose down under my ribs, I just had ter laff. Brer Coon, I swear ter goodness, I'm de most ticklish chap you ever laid your eyes on. 'Twan't de fightin', 'twuz de laffin' dat keeled me over. Dat's why 'twuz dat you got de furst chance ter bust inter Brer Fox . . . but if it hadn't been dat I wuz ticklish, I'd a-knocked de breff outer his body before you could say *slam-bang!*"

Brer Coon scratch his head. Den he look at Brer Possum right hard, an de cornders of his mouf turned up in a grin. "Brer Possum," he say, "when it comes ter fightin', you is mighty back-erds about comin' forerds. But when it comes ter makin' up excuses fer *not* fightin', you is not backerds at all."

Wid dat, Brer Coon run straight home an tell Mrs. Coon all dat Brer Possum say. Mrs. Coon, she tell Miss Mink, an Miss Mink, she tell Miss Goose. Miss Goose tell Mr. Rooster, an he went round an round de neighborhood, tellin' de story everywhers. An down ter dis day, wheresomever der's pretendin' goin' on, like somebody actin' dead when he ain't dead at all, folks call it "Playin' Possum."

Brer Rabbit an de Gizzard-Eater

ONE EVENIN', Brer Rabbit wuz invited ter a Halloween party, way over across de river. Whiles he wuz der, toastin' marshmellers an bobbin' fer apples, a great rain poured down. By de time Brer Rabbit left de party, it wuz late in de night. Now de rainin' had stopped, but de river wuz all swoll up. De bridge wuz broke an de ferry wuz-zent runnin'.

Brer Rabbit sot down on de river-bank, tryin'

ter study out a way ter go across, an get home. He study an study. Dat river look wide, an de water in it look like de deepest, wettest water he ever laid eyes on. Brer Rabbit don't like it. "Maybe somebody round here got a boat!" he say ter hisself. "I'll call out an ask!"

"Hey! Heyo!" he holler inter de darkness. "Hallo! Anybody got a boat? Heyo! Hey!"

Nobody answer.

Brer Rabbit holler again, den again. He holler

so loud an so long, dat he woke up Brer Alligater, stretched out on his muddy bed in de river grass, just below.

"Who is dat makin' all dat racket up der?" he shout. "What do you want?"

"It's Brer Rabbit. I want a boat!"

"Brer Rabbit, eh? Well, what you want a boat fer at dis time of night?" Brer Alligater crawl out from his bed, an rise up ter de top of de water. He float der, backerds and forerds, like he don't weigh no more dan a fedder.

"I want a boat ter carry me 'cross dis wet river," say Brer Rabbit.

"Too bad! Der ain't no boat here! But wait a minute now, I tell you what I'll do, Brer Rabbit. I'll carry you 'cross de river myself."

Brer Rabbit, he sorter surprised at dis, cause he ain't exactly what you might call a friend of Brer Alligater, an der ain't never been any lovin' wurds nor Chrismas presents circulatin' round twixt de Rabbit an de Alligater fambly. Howsomever, Brer Rabbit want ter get across dat river mighty bad.

"Thankee, Brer 'Gater," he say. "Just how deep is dat water what you're floatin' in?"

"Dis river is so deep," Brer 'Gater answer, "dat if you wuz ter fall in right now, 'twould be termorrer mawnin' before you'd touch de bottom."

Dis make Brer Rabbit feel like he goin' ter faint dead away. "Well, er, Brer 'Gater," he say, "how you figgerin' ter take me across dis deep river?"

Brer 'Gater, he blow a bubble er two outer his nose. "I'll carry you across on my back, of course."

Brer Rabbit, he think an he think, an de more he think, de more he don't like dis idea. But he got ter get ter de other side of dat river. "Brer 'Gater," he say, "I believe I'll accep' your invitation an go along wid you. Please be so kind ez ter drive yourself up a little closer ter de bank, so's I won't slip whilst I'm gettin' on."

Brer 'Gater, he drift up by de side of de bank, an float der, wid his two eyes shinin' like little red lights, an a big broad smile on his face.

Now Brer Rabbit notice dat when dat Alligater smile, his mouf had a double row of monstus sharp toofs, dat stretched all de way back ter his ears. Dis make Brer Rabbit shake an shiver like he havin' a chill. He look up; he look down; he look all around, but he don't see no boat, nor no floatin' log ter help him get across dat river. He don't see nothin' exceptin' dat Alligater. "Brer 'Gater," he say, "your back is rough wid bumps an humps. How am I goin' ter ride it?"

"Easy!" say Brer 'Gater. "Just fit your foots on de bumps and de humps an brace yourself. Den, just set der easy, like you wuz ridin' a water-hoss."

Well suh, Brer Rabbit got on. But he no sooner got on, dan he wished mighty hard he wuz off. Dat Alligater, he slip throo de water like he wuz greased. Now of course, Brer Rabbit keep his eyes wide open, an purty soon he notice dat Brer Alligater wuzn't steerin' fer de other side of de river at all. He wuz steerin' fer some place way far off in de dark. "Why, dis Alligater's up ter something!" he say ter hisself.

"What's de matter wid you, Brer 'Gater? You ain't steerin' very well," he sing out. "Or maybe you fergot you wuz takin' me across ter de other side of de river."

"Fergot?" snort Brer 'Gater. "I ain't fergot nothin'!" Now Brer 'Gater turn his head all de way round an grin at Brer Rabbit. "Espeshally, I ain't fergot dat day you sot de grass afire down here by de river, an I got burnt. Dat's de reason my back is so rough, Brer Rabbit, an dat's de reason I been waitin' fer you. I been waitin' a long, long time. Well . . . now I got you." Brer 'Gater open up his great mouf, an he laff.

When Brer Rabbit look down inter dat big open alligater mouf, it seem like he see more toofs dan der wuz stars in de sky. Den he look down at de deep, dark water gurglin' all around. Brer Rabbit trimble. He can't speak a wurd,

cause de cold fear wuz clutchin' at his windpipe.

Brer 'Gater, he keep on laffin', an slippin' along throo de water. "Brer Rabbit," he say, "I'm takin' you way, way off ter de slippery, sloppery slushes, an when I get der, I'm goin' ter goozle out your gizzard."

Right den, Brer Rabbit's thinkin' machine start wurkin' faster dan if de lightenin' struck it. He clear up his throat, an he kinder chuckle. "Well! If it's a gizzard dat you want, it's a mighty lucky thing you met up wid me!"

Now Brer 'Gater sorter puzzled, cause he wuzn't expectin' ter hear Brer Rabbit chuckle; he wuz expectin' ter hear him boo-hoo. "Lucky? What do you mean, lucky?"

"Just dis, Brer 'Gater; since it's a gizzard you want, I've got something worf your while. I ain't got just one gizzard. I got two!"

"*Two gizzards!*" Now Brer 'Gater turrible puzzled, an he kinder curious about Brer Rabbit's two gizzards. "Why you got two? How come dat?"

"I dunno *why*, Brer 'Gater . . . all I knows is dat I got um."

"Well, you ain't goin' ter have um very long," say Brer 'Gater, "cause I'm goin' ter goozle um out."

"I'm afraid you can't do dat," say Brer Rabbit, "cause I ain't got my gizzards here."

"*You ain't got um here!*" Now Brer 'Gater get-

63

tin' so curious about dose two gizzards he begin ter ferget bein' so mad. "Why . . . why . . . what in de wurld do you mean, Brer Rabbit? You mean you took your gizzards out an left um somewhers?"

Brer Rabbit snicker, actin' like he think Brer 'Gater wuz just a numbskull sorter creetur. "Course I took my gizzards out. It's Halloween! Whoever heard of a rabbit goin' ter a Halloween party wid his gizzards in?"

Now Brer 'Gater so crazy-puzzled his mind wuz all mixed up. He don't understand about dis gizzard bizness, an he ain't never been invited ter a Halloween party, so he don't suspicion dat Brer Rabbit wuz up ter any trick. "Well, Brer Rabbit," he say, "wher—wher'd you leave your gizzards when you took um out?"

"I hid um, Brer 'Gater, right over der—in de trunk of a big holler tree." Brer Rabbit point throo de dark towards de woods on de other side of de river, just wher he wanted ter go.

Well suh, Brer 'Gater, he can't wait another minute ter get hold of dose gizzards. He whirl round in de water, an he steer fer de woods, swimmin' along fast ez he can.

Soon ez dey get close up ter de land, Brer Rabbit make a jump fer de dry, solid ground. "Come on, Brer 'Gater!" he yell. "Dis is de way! Just foller me!" An wid dat, Brer Rabbit just disappeared inter de dark.

Brer 'Gater, he scramble up de bank, but of course he ain't fast enuff ter foller Brer Rabbit. Right away, he get lost. An fer all I know, dat Alligater is still thrashin' round dose woods somewhers, huntin' fer Brer Rabbit, a holler tree, and de two rabbit gizzards dat ain't der.

De Whipme-Whopme Puddin'

Many's de long time ago, der wuz a Man dat lived in de same neighborhood ez de creeturs. Der wan't nothin' queer about dis Man; he wuz just a plain, everyday kinder Man wid a farm. He had a cabbige patch, an a barley patch, and he growed a bit of wheat an corn. On top of dat, he had a yard full of chickens, an der's wher de trouble began.

Every time de creeturs run by dat yard, der moufs began ter water. De hens wuz plump; de pullets wuz fat; an de fryin'-size chicks look like dey want ter hop right inter de pan. Now when dat's de case, what you reckon goin' ter happen? Brer Fox want chicken; Brer Bear want chicken; Brer Rabbit want chicken; an dey all set der minds ter figgerin' how ter get it. But 't wan't easy, cause de Man kept de gate ter de chicken-yard locked.

Whiles Brer Fox an Brer Bear wuz just sittin' round arguin' how ter get in, Brer Rabbit wuz already hard at wurk. He brung a bag, an he hid it in de bushes just outside de chicken-yard fence. Den, every night, he just went an sot der,

waitin' fer dat sometime when Mr. Man might forget ter lock up.

By-m-by dat sometime come. One dark Sunday night, Mr. Man had some friends come ter call. De lights in de house wuz all on, de dog wuz inside, an dey wuz eatin' an drinkin' an kickin' up such a racket dat dey couldn't a-heard it if de whole house had blowed down. Mr. Man, he don't have a thought in his head 'bout de yard gate bein' unlocked, an de chicken house door wide open.

Well, dat night, Brer Rabbit wuz right on hand. Long about midnight he pick up de bag dat he'd brung, an he walk right in de yard. He scoop up de chickens, ez many ez he can, an dump um inter de bag. Dey kinder cluck an flutter, but dey don't make too much fuss. Den he fling de bag across his shoulders an off he scaddle home, sassy an gay ez can be.

Mrs. Rabbit, she cooked de chickens, an de Rabbit fambly ate up every bit. Now of course, de chickens, bein' all eat up, wuz all outer sight, but de fedders, dey wuz still around. Mrs. Rabbit, she want ter burn um in de fire.

"No," say Brer Rabbit. "De whole neighbor-hood'll smell um. I got a better way dan dat." So, de next mawnin' after brekfus, he stuff de fedders inter his bag, an he start off down de road.

After a while, he pass by Brer Bear's house an he see him sittin' der, a-smokin' his pipe on de porch. Brer Rabbit yell, "Howdy," an he just walk on.

"Hey!" call out Brer Bear. "What you got in dat bag?"

"Oh—just some stuff I'm takin' ter de mill ter get grinded. It sure is a long walk ter dat mill."

Wid dat, Brer Rabbit sot de bag down by de side of de road, an wipe his face wid his hank-cher.

Brer Bear, he come down off de porch ter wher Brer Rabbit wuz settin'. "What kinder stuff you takin' ter de mill? Is it corn, or wheat?"

Brer Rabbit kinder roll his eyes mysterious-like. "Oh, 't ain't neither."

"Well," say Brer Bear, "den what is it?"

Brer Rabbit look round like he wanter make sure nobody wuz lissenin'. Den he whisper, "It's very valubble, Brer Bear. It's Winniannimus grass. Soon ez de miller get it grinded up, it'll be worf ten dollars a pound."

Dis make Brer Bear sorter prick up his ears. "Winniannimus grass? What's dat?"

"Don't you know 'bout Winniannimus grass?" Brer Rabbit act real surprised. "Why, Winnian-nimus grass is de grass dat rich folks buys when dey wants ter make Whipme-Whopme puddin'."

Now of course Brer Bear never heard of Whipme-Whopme puddin', but any kind of pud-din' dat rich folks likes, sound purty good ter him. He want ter go along ter de mill too, an get a taste of dis fancy grass, soon ez de miller get it grinded. So, he pick up de bag, an say he be pleased ter carry it, seein' ez how Brer Rabbit been walkin' so far an feelin' sorter tired.

67

Well suh, dey go along tergedder, till after a while, Brer Rabbit look back, an he seed Brer Fox a-comin'. Dis make him chuckle ter hisself, cause now he know dat purty soon he goin' ter have a powerful big laff. Now he pretend dat he just teetotally tired out. He pant an mop his face again. "Brer Bear," he say, "I got ter set right down here an take a rest, but you just go on ahead, an I'll join you in a little while up at de mill."

"Shucks, Brer Rabbit! You tired already? Guess you ain't ez sprucy dese days ez I is." Brer Bear fro out his chest, an he trot on along wid de bag.

Brer Rabbit, he squot down on his hunkers an wait till Brer Fox come along. "Howdy, Brer Fox!" he sing out. "Why, just dis minute, Brer Bear passed by here, askin' if I done seed you anywhers. Der he goes, dat's him up de road der wid de bag on his back."

"So 'tis," say Brer Fox. "What's he got in de bag?"

"He say it some kinder grass dat he takin' ter de mill ter get grinded, but if you ask me, I seed a heap of chicken fedders stickin' out from a hole in de side."

"*Chicken fedders!* Why, dat low-down cheatin' thief! He done stole dose chickens from Mr.

Man's yard. He done beat me to um!" Wid dat, he race up de road, an he ketch up wid Brer Bear.

"What you got in dat bag?" he holler, shakin his walkin'-stick in Brer Bear's face.

"Just Winniannimus grass, Brer Fox . . . de kind dat makes de rich folks' Whipme-Whopme puddin'."

"I'll whip an whop *you*, you villyun!" holler Brer Fox. Wid dat, he up wid his walkin'-stick an he smack de bag. De chicken fedders, dey fly out. Den he up wid his walkin'-stick ter smack Brer Bear.

But Brer Bear, he don't get no whippin' nor no whoppin', cause right den Mr. Man come trompin' down de road. He see de fedders flutterin' throo de air an now he know'd who stole his chickens. Mr. Man let out one monstus big yell! Now Brer Fox an Brer Bear don't wait ter argue 'bout any Winniannimus grass. Dey scoot out from der like a hornet stung um, wid Mr. Man streakin' along right behind.

Brer Rabbit, he just sot der wher he wuz, a-lickin' his paws, till by-m-by, Brer Fox an Brer Bear wid Mr. Man after um done disappear inter a big cloud of dust, far, far away.

King Lion at de Water-Hole

ONCE DER WUZ a summertime dat wuz turrible dry, an drinkin' water fer de creeturs wuz turrible scarce. De river dried up, de brooks made der disappearance, an der wurn't nothin in de mill-pond exceptin' de old tree stumps dat grew der on de bottom. De only place left fer de creeturs ter drink at wuz de big spring right in de middle of de woods.

Now der wurn't nothin' wrong wid dis spring, an der should have been enuff water fer everbody, but it just so happened dat King Lion wanted ter have it all ter hisself. Every time any of de other creeturs come near dat spring, King Lion would jump out from de bushes, shake his mane, an let out a thunderin' roar. Den off would scurry de other creeturs faster dan a mess of punkins rollin' down hill, an King Lion would just go on drinkin' ez much ez he pleased.

Every day de creeturs got thirstier an thirstier. Soon ez de water wuz all gone, dey ate up all de fruits wid juices. Dey guzzle all de watermellions a-growin' on de vine. Dey gobble all de berries a-ripenin' on de branch. Dey scrunch de prickly cactus bush an suck out all de sap.

Brer Rabbit, he get so thirsty he lick de sticky pine juice off de pine trees. He even try ter chew de juice outer de grass an de weeds. An every night when de sun go down, he lay on de ground wid his mouf open wide, hopin' dat de dew will drop in. But it don't do no good. Brer Rabbit just get thirstier an thirstier, an he feel like he growin' fedders on his tongue.

By-m-by, Brer Rabbit get mad. "I want a drink, an I'm goin' ter have it right now," he say, "an no Lion ain't goin' ter stop me!" Wid dat, he prance off *lippity clippity*, straight ter de woods. Soon ez he get close up near de spring, he tiptoe

69

along sorter careful, an look round. Der wuz King Lion, sittin' right in de middle of dat clear, cool spring, just a-splishin' an a-splashin', an lettin' all dat wonderful wet water drip down from his great Kingy mane.

Brer Rabbit just can't stand it. "Look at him! Look at him!" he say ter hisself. "Sloshin' his big foots in dat spring, when de rest of us ain't got e'en one teenchy little drop ter drink! Look at him!"

Now Brer Rabbit put his mind right ter wurk. He squot down der in de bushes an he think an he think 'bout what he goin' ter do. He don't dare run down an just help hisself ter a moufful, cause dat Lion so big an so strong he can squash Brer Rabbit wid one flip of his paw. "Furst," say Brer Rabbit, "I got ter get King Lion ter come outer de water. Den, I got ter tie him up. An dat's not easy—no, not easy."

Brer Rabbit sot der a long time, turnin' his mind round an round. Purty soon, he notice dat a little breeze wuz comin' up. It wuz whiskin' throo de leaves on de ground, an rustlin' throo de leaves on de trees. Dis give Brer Rabbit just de idea he want!

Off he scamper home. Der, he fetch a big, strong rope. Den, back he skip ter de woods again, ter a place close by de spring.

Now Brer Rabbit ready. First, he take a deep bref. Den, he start ter run, fast ez he can. He puff an he pant like he been runnin' a long, long way. Soon ez he get near enuff ter de spring fer King Lion ter see him, he start ter holler an yell, *'Ooo! Ooo!* Look out! OOO!"

King Lion look up from wher he wuz waller-in' in de water. "Heyo, Brer Rabbit! What's de matter? Wher you goin' wid dat rope?"

"I'm goin' ter tie myself fast ter a tree," pant Brer Rabbit. Den he stop runnin' fer a minnit, like he can't ketch his bref. "You better tie your-self fast ter a tree too, King Lion. . . . Lissen ter dat wind . . . der's a hurrycane-storm blowin' up."

"A hurrycane-storm?" King Lion glance up, an sure enuff, he see some leaves flutterin' throo de air. Now King Lion skeered: "I ain't got no rope ter tie myself ter a tree. What am I goin' ter do?"

"Guess you better run, King Lion. Run real fast!"

"I'm too big an old ter run real fast, Brer Rabbit."

"Den dig a hole an bury yourself, King Lion. Dig a hole!"

"It takes a while ter dig a hole, Brer Rabbit. I ain't got time."

"Well, den," say Brer Rabbit, "I guess der ain't nothin' you can do. You'll just have ter sit der in de water an let de hurrycane blow you away." Now Brer Rabbit began ter onquoile his rope like he goin' ter tie hisself up ter a tree.

King Lion lissen ter de wind swishin' up de leaves an whistlin' throo de bushes, an he feel awful skeered. He trimble. His teef begin ter chatter an his great mane bristle up. Out he wade from de spring, thrashin' dis way an dat wid his tail. "Lend me a piece of your rope, Brer Rabbit," he beg. "Tie me up ter dat tree too!"

An dat's exactly what Brer Rabbit did. He take his rope an he tie King Lion so tight ter dat tree dat forty Elephents an a Rhinossyhoss couldn't have pulled him loose.

"Now dat's dat," say Brer Rabbit, an down he march ter de spring, an he fetch hisself a big, long drink. He drink an drink till he can't drink no more. Den back he march ter King Lion, an squot down beside him on his hunkers. He cross his legs, sorter careless like, an start washin' his face wid his paw.

King Lion watch him, an he notice dat he ain't hurryin' ter tie hisself up ter any tree. Den King Lion watch de leaves gently flutterin' throo de air, an he notice dat de wind ain't really blowin' so speshally bad. Now King Lion look down at de rope tied round his stummock an his legs an he know dat he been fooled. Wid dat, he start ter roar. He roar so loud dat all de creeturs in de neighborhood come rushin' ter see what de rukus wuz about.

Up jump Brer Rabbit. "Come on, folks . . . de coast is clear," he yell. "You is perfectly safe! Come down ter de spring an drink all you can. Look wher I got King Lion!"

And did dose creeturs come! De big ones an de little ones . . . de tall ones an de short ones, de fat ones an de scrawny ones . . . dey come pushin' an shovin' an scuffin' an scroogin' ter get der furst. And did dose creeturs drink! Dey lapped up dat deelicious cool spring water. Dey gulped it. Dey guzzled it. An between every moufful, dey said ter each other dat Brer Rabbit wuz de smartest little creetur in de whole wurld, cause he tied up dat powerful big Lion.

As fer King Lion, he just kept on roarin' an roarin', cause der wurn't nothin' else fer him ter do.

Judge Rabbit an Miss Grouse

ER WUZ one time way back yonder, when de creeturs, most speshally de birds, ain't had enuff ter do. An dey got ter quarrelin' an squabblin', just like folks do now. A gentermen-bird wouldn't stop ter say Howdy when he passed another gentermen-bird in de air, an even if he did, de other gentermen-bird would refuse ter Howdy back.

Whiles de gentermen-birds wuz carryin' on like dis, de lady-birds wuz just ez bad. Dey got ter wranglin' about der looks and der fedders, till it seemed like dey hatchin' up a really-truly war. Each one of um think she de purtiest, an each one of um strut round wid her chin in de air.

After a while de argument got so hot dat somethin' had ter be done, cause most of dese ladies had sharp bills, an some of um had claws. Miss Robin, Miss Wren an Miss Blue Bird, dey put der heads tergedder ter figger out how de argument goin' ter be stopped. But dey can't figger out a blessed thing.

By-m-by, little Miss Magpie speak up. She had a temper wid salt an pepper on it, an she wuz gettin cross an peevish. "Ladies," she say, snappin' her little sharp beak, "we got ter have a big meetin', a sorter contest, an all kinds an all colors of us lady-birds got ter come. We'll get a judge, an make him sot down an watch us while we parade. Den he'll pick de one dat's de purti-est—an de one dat he picks . . . well, she's de one. Den, we won't have ter argue no more."

De lady-birds, dey cackle an dey squawk, but dey like dis idea, an at Miss Quail's suggestion, dey chose Brer Rabbit ter be de judge.

Now of course Brer Rabbit wuzzent accustomed ter associatin' wid de feddered creeturs, espeshally feddered ladies widout much sense. Howsomever, he agreed ter do de judgin', providin' every single lady-bird wuz present, an every single lady-bird would agree ter accept de winner dat he picked.

"An if I say de Squinch Owl or de Buzzard is de purtiest," say Brer Rabbit, "den all you other birds got ter say so too."

'Twuz agreed.

When de day come fer de contest, Brer Rabbit wuz right on hand. He prance up in his Sunday pants an wescut, an he take his seat on de judge's stand. Den, de lady-birds, dey start struttin', an dey march along in front of him, one by one.

Brer Rabbit, he look um all over. He put on his specks an he look some more. Den he shake his head. "No, ladies, dis won't do. You is not all here. Miss Grouse ain't present. You is all got ter be in dis contest, every one, else you won't bide by my say-so, an you lady-birds will go on arguin' about who is de purtiest de rest of your life."

De birds, dey pouted. Dey jibbered an dey jabbered, an some say Miss Grouse ain't worf bodderin' wid, cause she's only a plain little nobody bird. Howsomever, dey start lookin' round mongst de bushes an de trees, an after a while, dey find her. Der she wuz, just stayin' at home, fixin' up some wurms fer de chilluns' supper.

"What's de matter wid you, Miss Grouse, grousin' round de house like dis?" say Miss Coo-Coo. "Ain't you comin' ter de beauty contest?"

"No," say Miss Grouse, "I ain't got nothin' ter wear."

"Shucks!" say Miss Coo-Coo. "Wear what you got on! Take a look at me in dis ole thing!" Miss Coo-Coo look down at de little bit of fuzz on her tail wher de fedders oughter be, an she sigh.

"No," say Miss Grouse, stampin' her little black foot. "I ain't goin' ter no beauty contest widout clothes."

De other birds, dey beg an dey beg, an by-m-by, Miss Grouse say she'll go if dey'd loan her some clothes. Well suh, dey all set ter wurk ter see what dey could lend her. Miss Cockatoo, she pull out a big yeller fedder from her top-knot; Miss Parrakeet, she pull out a long blue one from her tail. Miss Turtle-Dove, Miss Skylark, an Miss Pigeon, dey pull out little white ones from der wings. Den Ole Miss Ostrich say dat wid her bony neck, she ain't got a chance ter win anyhow, an she pull out a whole bunch of de purtiest fedders you ever did see.

Den, dey pinned de fedders on Miss Grouse.

Dey stuck a pink one here. Dey tucked a green one der. Dey shaped um an dey draped um. Dey curled um an dey twurled um, till purty soon, Miss Grouse wuz dressed up fit ter kill.

Now de lady-birds wuz all present, an dey come crowdin' back before de judge.

"Fall in line, you fancy bird-gals!" command Brer Rabbit from high up on de judge's stand.

De bird-gals did ez dey wuz told, an now de parade began. Miss Grouse, she lead de procession. Wid all dose borrered fedders, der wan't no two ways about it, she wuz de purtiest of de whole gang.

Brer Rabbit come down from de judge's stand wid a big red ribbon, an he pin it on her chest. "Miss Grouse," he say, "you is de best-lookin' bird-gal I ever set my eyes on. You is de winner of dis show."

De other lady-birds, dey giggle an dey gaggle, but dey all had ter agree dat Miss Grouse wuz de most beautiful lady-bird in de wurld. Now dat de matter wuz settled an dey didn't have ter argue no more, dey wuz all ez happy ez can be, all exceptin' Miss Grouse. She knew dat down under her fancy borrered fedders, she wuz just a plain little nobody bird, dat liked ter stay home an eat wurms.

75

Brer Rabbit's Laffin' Place

AFTER DE TIME dat Brer Rabbit tied up King Lion, he got ter feelin' high an mighty. "In all dis wurld," he brag, "der ain't no creetur dat dares ter lay his paws on me. I'm safe. I can go wheresomever, whensomever I please." An dis Brer Rabbit did. Every mawnin', soon ez he'd shuck de dew off his tail, off he'd go a-prankin' round de neighborhood, widout a thought in his head about bein' ketched.

'Twan't long before Brer Rabbit began ter grow a bit careless.

Well, one afternoon, he happened ter feel sorter tired. So, all by his own alone self, he hop off ter de woods ter take a little nap. He lay down, right in de broad open daytime, an he snooze an he snooze. He don't know exactly how long he snooze, but by-m-by, he hear a mumblin' an a mutterin' close beside him. Brer Rabbit wiggle his nose. He open up his eyes just a slit. Lo an behold, he see dat he ain't in de woods any more at all! He's somewhere way down in de dark insides of a cave. Der's a fire cracklin' der in de darkness, an poppin' out red sparks.

Brer Rabbit stretch his eyes open wide. He look ter one side, an who does he see, gnashin' his shiny sharp teef, but de last person on dis earf he want ter see—dat meanest of all persons, BRER FOX! He look ter de other side, an who does he see, grinnin' right down in his face, but de next meanest of all persons, BRER BEAR! Brer Rabbit so skeered his heart go *flip, flup!*

Now he look down at hisself, an what does he see but a great big ROPE, tied round an round him, all de way from his foots ter his chin! Wurse dan dat, he's tied up tight ter a stick, like a ear of green corn, all ready ter roast! Brer Rabbit not feelin' high an mighty any more. Brer Rabbit so skeered de chills go runnin' down his back, all de way out ter de end of his little bob-tail.

Brer Fox, he lean down close ter Brer Rabbit an snarl his teef. "I ketched you dis time, Brer Rabbit. I ketched you fer sure!" He twist de rope tighter round Brer Rabbit's neck, an he tie it in a knot. Den he wink at Brer Bear. "Look, Brer Bear, I'm goin' ter make dis little Rabbit a bow necktie!" Now he jerk de rope—brrrppp! Brer Rabbit's bref come quick. His neck is almost squoze.

Brer Bear laff. "You look mighty slick in dat bow tie, Brer Rabbit. You is all dressed up fer dinner!"

"My dinner!" say Brer Fox. He lick his chops.

"My dinner too! Mmm . . . mmm!" say Brer Bear, smackin' his lips. "Take a look at dat fire, Brer Rabbit. Dat's wher we're goin' ter roast you. We're goin' ter roast you right now."

Brer Rabbit see de red-hot flames leapin' up from de fire, an he skeered most outer his skin. If ever der wuz a time he had ter wurk his mind fast, dat time wuz den. He wurk it an wurk it, an by-m-by it fetch him just de right idea.

Well suh, Brer Rabbit, he open his mouf, an he laff very loud. "Ha-ha-ha!"

Brer Fox an Brer Bear, dey so 'stonished dey look at each other like dey wuz struck dumb. Brer Fox clear up his throat. "Maybe you didn't hear me, Brer Rabbit," he shout. "I said we're goin' ter *roast* you."

Brer Rabbit laff some more.

"I guess you don't understand," holler Brer Bear. "We said we're goin' ter ROAST YOU ON DIS BURNIN' FIRE! Dat's nothin' ter laff at! You ought ter be skeered!"

Brer Rabbit laff some more an some more. "I heard you say you're goin' ter roast me!"

"But why you laffin'!" ask Brer Fox.

"Excuse me Brer Fox, but I just can't help laffin', cause I just been ter my laffin' place."

"Laffin' place?" Brer Bear scratch his head. "What's a laffin' place?"

"Oh, it's a secret place I know about," say Brer Rabbit.

"Hmmmm, a secret place," Brer Fox grumble ter hisself. "I'd sorter like ter know about dat secret place. Tell me what 'tis, Brer Rabbit. Don't you sassy me—tell me what 'tis dis very minute!"

But Brer Rabbit just laff some more an some more an some more. Den he say, "I can't tell you exactly what 'tis. I'd have ter show you, but how can I show you when I'm all tied up like dis?" Now de laffs come so hard dat Brer Rabbit look like he goin' ter shake his jaw bones loose.

Brer Fox and Brer Bear, dey watch him, an dey get curiouser an curiouser ter know what dat secret laffin' place is. Dey go off ter a cornder of de cave, an dey whisper tergedder. Den, dey come back.

"Brer Rabbit," say Brer Fox, shakin' his paw right smack in Brer Rabbit's face, "we want you ter take us ter dat secret laffin' place of yours. But soon ez we see what 'tis, an where 'tis, back you're comin' ter dis cave. Den, we'll hurry up wid de roastin'."

Wid dat, dey take Brer Rabbit down from de stick. Dey unwind de rope, but dey keep him tied on ter one end.

Den dey start off. Brer Fox an Brer Bear, dey march along sorter serious-like, hangin' on tight

77

ter de rope. Brer Rabbit, he lead de way ter de woods, prancin' an dancin', like bein' tied ter a rope wuz a fine lot of fun.

By-m-by, dey get ter a place wher der wuz a big hick'ry tree, wid a sorter holler place in de trunk. When Brer Rabbit see dat, he start ter laff again, an de haw-haws come bustin' outer his mouf so fast dat he can't skacely stand on his foots. "Der 'tis!" he yell, pointin' ter de tree. "Der's my laffin' place, right der!"

"I don't see nothin' ter laff at," say Brer Fox.

"Nor me," say Brer Bear. "I don't feel funny at all!"

"You will," say Brer Rabbit. "Step up closer ter de holler in dat tree. Den poke your heads way, way down inside!"

Well, Brer Fox an Brer Bear, dey did exactly dat, but it didn't make um feel exactly funny.

Brer Fox let out a howl.

"Yeouch! Yeouch!" squall Brer Bear. Den out from de tree come bofe der heads, an out come a hundred thousand bumbly-bees! Dey swarm round Brer Fox an Brer Bear. Dey sting um. Dey bite um like dey goin' ter tear der hides clean off. Brer Fox an Brer Bear, dey whack um an dey smack um, an dey ferget ter hold on ter Brer Rabbit's rope. Dey ferget everything except battin' dose bees.

By-m-by, de bees get tired, an dey go away.

Now Brer Fox an Brer Bear sit down ter ketch der bref. Der heads wuz all swell up; der eyes wuz squinched up tight; an dey wuz mighty mad. Just den, from de bushes right behind um, dey hear a sorter snicker. Brer Rabbit!

Brer Bear, he foam at de mouf.

Brer Fox, he chomp his teef. "Why—you—you slinkin' low-down Watchermacollum! You said dis wuz a laffin' place!"

"I said 'twuz MY laffin' place," sing out Brer Rabbit. "Dis is de best laff I ever had!" Wid dat, he fro back his head an he let out such a whoopin' big laff dat it echo all throo de woods, an down throo de gopher tunnels, under de ground.

De Birds in de trees, dey hear him an dey start laffin' too, den dé Squirrels, de Woodchucks, de Weasels an de Wurms. Purty soon, every creetur in de woods wuz laffin' fit ter kill—all except Brer Fox an Brer Bear, an dey didn't laff at all.

De Great Rabbit-Terrapin Race

ONE MAWNIN', Brer Rabbit wuz goin' *lippity clippity* down de road, and he wuz feelin' gay an mighty sassy. He prance, and he dance. He wink at de daisies a-growin' in de fields. He bow ter de tall, hansome trees and say Howdy ter de crickets an de bees. By-m-by, he feel so gay he have ter turn a summersault.

Just den, along come Brer Terrapin. "Heyo, Brer Rabbit! What in de wurld is de matter wid you, caperin' round like dis right in de middle of de road?"

"Der ain't nothin' de matter wid me," sing out Brer Rabbit. "I feel fine! Why shouldn't I feel fine? I'm de smartest creetur on dis earf!"

Brer Terrapin nod his head. "Dat you is, Brer Rabbit."

"I'm de smartest, an I'm de fastest, too!" Now Brer Rabbit have ter turn another summersault, an another, an another.

Brer Terrapin watch him fer a bit, an den he think ter hisself, "I like dis Rabbit. We always been good friends. But now he's gettin' too stuck-up, braggin' dat he's de smartest, an de fastest too. Dat ain't good. No, dat ain't good. I got ter do somethin' about dat."

An so Brer Terrapin did. Soon ez Brer Rabbit stop turnin' summersaults, Brer Terrapin up'n say, "What you mean, braggin' you're de fastest creetur on dis earf?"

Brer Rabbit jump up. "Dat ain't braggin'. Of course I'm de fastest! Who says I ain't?"

"Who says so?" Brer Terrapin grin round de cornders of his mouf. "*I* say you ain't de fastest. *I* is."

"*You . . . you* de fastest!" Brer Rabbit bust out laffin'. "Wid dose fat, short legs? Wid dat thick shell? Why, you can't run . . . you can't skacely even *crawl!*"

"Is dat so?" Brer Terrapin sorter snicker. "Oh, you can skip along purty fast fer a short ways, but when it comes ter a long ways, I'm de one dat'll get der furst every time."

Well, dey went on arguin' like dis fer quite a while. Den Brer Terrapin say he got a bag of gold buried under a rock down at de bottom of de pond, an dat Brer Rabbit can have it, if he can beat him in a race. Brer Rabbit say he got a bag of gold hidden in his chimbley, an Brer Terrapin can have dat, if he can beat him. 'Twuz agreed dat de race would be three miles, an dat dey'd ask Brer Tukkey Buzzard ter be de judge.

Brer Buzzard, he laff an sorter fuzzle up his fedders when dey told him 'bout de race, cause he sure Brer Rabbit wuz goin' ter win. Howsomever, he agreed ter be de judge, an dey gave him de two bags of gold ter hold fer de winner.

Furst, Brer Buzzard measure off de ground wher de race wuz ter be runned. He marked off a startin' line an a finishin' line. An at de end of every mile, he stuck up a post. Den he explained de rules:

"You have ter start at de startin' line, an at de end of each mile, you have ter touch one of dese posts. Den, you have ter finish at de finishin' line. Dese is de rules, but you can run whersomever you like, on de road in de sunshine, or throo de woods in de shade."

"I'll take de road in de sunshine," say Brer Rabbit.

"I'll take de woods in de shade," say Brer Terrapin.

Brer Buzzard say de race would be next Chuseday, an he invited all de creeturs ter come.

Brer Rabbit, he can't skacely wait. All day, every day, he just sit an watch de clock a-clockin' on de mantlepiece, waitin' fer Chuseday ter come. Ez fer old Brer Terrapin, he just lay low on de bottom of de pond wid Mrs. Terrapin an der two chilluns, whisperin' an cookin' up a plan fer how ter win.

Den at last, dat Chuseday come. Early in de mawnin', soon ez de sun come up outer hidin',

Brer Terrapin an his fambly crawl out from de pond, an shuffle off ter de woods. Purty soon de other creeturs begin ter arrive. Brer Fox, Brer Wolf, Brer Bear, Brer Coon, Sis Possum, Sis Cow, dey all arrive, chucklin' an gigglin' mongst demselves, cause dey think de race is sorter silly, bein' ez how Brer Rabbit's bound ter win. Howsomever, dey take der places close-by de finishin' line. Den, Brer Buzzard come floppin' along, swingin' de two bags of gold. Now up prance Brer Rabbit, all dressed up fit ter kill, wid a red satin bow tied round his neck, an a green one round each of his ears.

Brer Buzzard hop up ter de startin' line, an pull out his watch. "Gentermens, is you ready?"

"Ready!" say Brer Rabbit, steppin' up ter de line.

"Ready!" say a voice from de woods, an a Terrapin step up ter de line. Now it just so happened dat all de Terrapin fambly wuz de very spittin' image of Brer Terrapin, so neither Brer Buzzard nor Brer Rabbit took notice dat 'twuz Mrs. Terrapin, an not Brer Terrapin, dat stepped up ter dat startin' line.

"On your mark!" shout Brer Buzzard. "Get set! Go!"

Brer Rabbit, he race off down de road. Mrs. Terrapin, she scramble off inter de woods. Brer Rabbit, he run fast ez he can, but just ez he get

almost ter de first mile post, what does he see but a Terrapin crawl outer de woods an touch it first! Brer Rabbit frown. "How'd you get here first?" he holler.

"Easy!" de Terrapin answer, an back he crawl inter de woods. Of course Brer Rabbit don't know dis is just one of de Terrapin chillun; natchally, he think it Brer Terrapin hisself.

Brer Rabbit, he gallop on. De dust fly high, but just as he get almost ter de second mile post, again, he seed a Terrapin crawl outer de woods an touch it first. Now Brer Rabbit mad. " 'T ain't possible!" he pant. "*I'm* de fastest creetur on dis earf!"

"You WUZ de fastest creetur!" de Terrapin answer, an off he skaddle ter de woods. Of course Brer Rabbit don't know dat dis is just de second of de Terrapin chillun; natchally, he think it Brer Terrapin hisself.

Brer Rabbit rush on. Dis wuz de last mile! He just tear up dat road like de dogs wuz after him, but it don't do no good. Just as he come puffin' up ter de finish line, Brer Terrapin hisself come amblin' out from de woods, an cross dat finish line first.

"Brer Terrapin's de winner!" yell all de creeturs.

"He is! Brer Terrapin *is* de winner!" yell Brer Buzzard, an he hand him de two bags of gold.

"Hooray fer Brer Terrapin!" De creeturs wave der paws; dey stomp an thomp de ground wid der tails. Den dey look at Brer Rabbit, huffin' an puffin' an kivvered wid dust, an dey laff.

Brer Rabbit, he pull de red bow off his neck, an de green bows off his ears, an he look sorter sollum. Den he go home ter Mrs. Rabbit. An all dat night, dey just sot in der chairs by de fire, drinkin' sassyfras tea, puzzlin' and puzzlin' about Brer Terrapin bein' de winner. Powerful puzzled dey wuz, cause of course, dey bofe know dat der ain't no faster creetur on dis earf dan Brer Rabbit.

Brer Bear Ketches Mr. Bull-Frog

EVERY NIGHT when Brer Bear went ter bed, he could hear de ole Bull-frogs a-blowin' bubbles an a-talkin' ter each other, down at de bottom of de pond. Every night Brer Bear lissen an try ter understand, but de more talk he hear, de less talk he understand. By-m-by he get ter lissenin' so hard he can't sleep at all. He just lay der tossin' an turnin' an rastlin' de kivers around.

Mrs. Bear, she can't stand it. One night, she get sorter cross. "Go ter sleep!" she say. "What's de matter wid you, anyway?"

"Hush up," whisper Brer Bear. "Lissen, do you hear dat?"

"Hear what?"

"Dat talk, dat *Jug-er-rum-kum-dum*. What's dat mean?"

"It don't mean nothin'. Dat's just Bull-frog talk." Mrs. Bear yawn. "Don't bodder me any more. Go ter sleep."

"Shhhhhh!" whisper Brer Bear. "Dey're sayin' it again, *Jug-er-rum-kum-dum! Jug-er-rum-kum-dum!* Dat surely must mean somethin'."

"I tell you it don't mean nothin'. Dat's just Bull-frog talk. In de nighttime, Bull-frogs all talk dat way. Now go ter sleep." Mrs. Bear, she turn her back, an soon she begin ter snore.

Brer Bear, he can't close his eyes all de long night. He just lay der tryin' ter understand what de Bull-frogs wuz sayin', an gettin' madder an madder all de time.

Soon ez de mornin' sun poke its head inter de sky, he get up. "Maybe dat *Jug-er-rum-kum-dum* talk mean somethin', an maybe it don't,"

83

he say, "but I'm goin' ter find out right now." Wid dat, he put on his pants an he march straight down ter de pond.

When he get der, lo an behold, who should he see settin' out on de bank sound asleep, but ole Brer Bull-frog hisself. Brer Bear creep up. He reach out wid his paw an he grab him. Now Brer Bull-frog wuz all scooped up in de palm of Brer Bear's paw.

Brer Bear look down an study him fer a minute. Den he say, "Now I've ketched you, Brer Bull-frog, an you're goin' ter sot right der in my paw, till you tell me what's de meanin' of dat talk you talk in de nighttime, down at de bottom of de pond."

Brer Bull-frog, he so skeered he can't hardly clear up his throat ter speak. "Whhh—whhhhh— what do you mean, what talk?"

"You know very well what I mean, dat *Jug-er-rum-kum-dum* talk." Brer Bear frown. "What's dat mean?"

"I can't tell you Brer Bear. I swear ter goodness I can't."

Now Brer Bear wrinkle up his forehead in a turrible scowl. "You tell me what dat *Jug-er-rum-kum-dum* talk means, an you tell me dis very minute."

Brer Bull-frog trimble an shake. "But I can't tell you now, Brer Bear, cause it don't mean nothin' in de daytime. It only means somethin' in de nighttime."

Dis make Brer Bear so mad he clinch de fist dat wuz holdin' Brer Bull-frog, till he almost squush de bref right outer him. "You're makin' fun of me," he holler, "an dat's just what you're doin' every night down at de bottom of de pond. But you ain't goin' make fun of me no more, cause I'm goin' do away wid you dis very minute." Wid dat, Brer Bear take his other paw an pick up a stick.

Brer Bull-frog, he start ter cry an boo-hoo. "Oh please, please Brer Bear, let me go, oh please!"

"No!" say Brer Bear, wavin' de stick. "I'm goin' ter make you inter Bull-frog hash before you have a chance ter make fun of me once more!"

Now Brer Bull-frog know dat somethin' have ter be done mighty quick. He sorter stop his boo-hooin' an he say, "Please, Brer Bear, if you're goin' ter kill me, first carry me out ter dat big flat rock, so's I can see my fambly just once more. Den, after I see um, you can take your stick an make me inter hash."

Brer Bear, he see de big tears rollin' down Brer Bull-frog's face, an he think ter hisself dat maybe it won't do no harm ter let him see his fambly just once more. So he wade out ter de rock. When he get der, he hold Brer Bull-frog

84

by de behind leg, an stretch him out on de top of de rock, near de edge, so's he can look down inter de water. Brer Bull-frog look way, way down. Den he sigh, like he settin' his eyes on his wife an chilluns fer de last time.

Brer Bear, he take a long bref, an he swing back his stick. It start ter come down, but just den, he hear a kinder hoarse rumblin' in Brer Bull-frog's throat. "*Jug-er-rum-kum-dum!*" he croak.

"*Jug-er-rum-kum-dum!*" croak all de Bull-frogs in de Bull-frog fambly. Dey jump up outer de water, an dey jump up on Brer Bear. Dey jump on his head, dey jump on his back, dey sit on his ears, dey slide down his nose. Der wuz hundreds an hundreds of Bull-frogs in dat Bull-frog fambly, an every last one of um wuz jumpin' some place on Brer Bear.

Brer Bear back away, thrashin' dis way an dat wid his arms. He let go Brer Bull-frog. He let go his stick. "Help! Help!" he yell. He slosh throo de water, an he scramble up de bank. Den off he skaddle, fast ez he can, back home ter Mrs. Bear.

Ez fer Brer Bull-frog an his fambly, dey just dive down ter de bottom of de pond. An dat night, an every night, dey just keep on sayin' *Jug-er-rum-kum-dum, Jug-er-rum-kum-dum,* like dey always did. An dat night, an every night, Brer Bear get madder dan de night before, cause now he really sure dose Bull-frogs is makin' fun of him.

Brer Rabbit Visits de Witch

AFTER DE TIME dat Brer Terrapin won de runnin' race, Brer Rabbit got ter feelin' sorter droopy. He worry an worry about how anyone can beat him, when he hisself is de fastest creetur on dis earf. He worry so much dat after a while, he feared he losin' de use of his mind. He feared de other creeturs would take ter foolin' him, an dat he ain't smart enuff ter fool um back. Wurse dan dat, he feared dat de bigger creeturs soon would ketch him, an skin him, an nail up his hide on de door.

"What in de name of goodness is de matter wid you?" ask Mrs. Rabbit one mawnin' when Brer Rabbit won't even get up outer bed.

Brer Rabbit don't answer.

Mrs. Rabbit try ter roust him up, but he won't be rousted. He just pull de kivvers up round his ears, an lay der like he wuz dead. De chilluns, dey beg der Daddy ter play hoppum-skippum, an piggy-back, but he just say, "Shoo! . . . Go 'way!" Brer Rabbit don't want ter do nothin'. He mope.

Mrs. Rabbit, she sit beside de bed. "You got

de mopes," she say. "You got ter go ter de Rabbit-Doctor an get yourself a pill."

Brer Rabbit don't want ter go ter any Doctor, but he do ez Mrs. Rabbit say.

"What's de trubble, Brer Rabbit?" ask de Rabbit-Doctor, when he see Brer Rabbit come shufflin' ter his door. "You're lookin' kinder weak. Ain't you feelin' well?"

"I got de mopes," say Brer Rabbit.

De Rabbit-Doctor, he take Brer Rabbit's paw an he lissen ter de tick-a-tickin' in his wrist. Den he make Brer Rabbit stick out his tongue, an he look way down inter his windpipe somewhers. "Hmmmm hmmmmmm!" he say, openin' his eye up big. "De mopes! Dat's exactly what it is." Den he give Brer Rabbit a box of green pills.

Brer Rabbit grunt, an he take de box, but he ain't de sort fer swallerin' pills. On de way back home, he fro um ter de ducks, an he watch um grabble up every one.

Well suh, Brer Rabbit don't get any better. He get wusser an wusser every day.

"You're gettin' thin an puny!" cry Mrs. Rabbit, wipin' a tear from her eye. "So thin an so puny, dat a teenchy little grasshopper could whack you down an carry you away!"

Now, Mrs. Rabbit know dat somethin' just had ter be done. She tell Brer Rabbit he got ter take a journey. He got ter go ask what's de matter from ole Aunt Mammy-Bammy Big-Money, de Witch-Rabbit, way, way off in de swamp. Wid dat, Mrs. Rabbit pack up a bag. Dat night, soon ez de dark begun ter drop down, she start Brer Rabbit along on his way.

It wuz a long, long way ter de middle of de deep, black swamp where Aunt Mammy-Bammy Big-Money lived. Dose dat wanted ter go der had ter jump some, hump some; hop some, flop some; ride some, slide some; creep some, leap some; foller some, holler some—an if dey wurn't mighty keerful, dey didn't get der den. Yet Brer Rabbit, he got der. When he smell de thick smoke comin' up throo a hole in de ground, he know dat's de place wher de Witch-Rabbit live.

Brer Rabbit squot down in de darkness an look round. He feel sorter skeered an trimbly. He feel hot, den he feel cold. De wind begin ter blow. It blow throo his ears, *buzz-zoo-o-o-o-o!*

It wissel throo de low swampy grass, *bizzy-bizzy-bzz-bzz!* Brer Rabbit skeerder an skeerder. He dasn't skacely wink his eye. Now de smoke wuz comin' up thicker an thicker, an he know 'twuz time fer him ter speak.

"Oh, Aunt Mammy-Bammy Big Money!" he cry. "It's Brer Rabbit! I come ter get your help!"

De voice of de Witch-Rabbit come oozlin' up throo de ground. "Why so, Brer Rabbit? Why so?"

"I'm losin' de use of my mind, Aunt Mammy-Bammy Big-Money! Der ain't no smartness in me any more. I'm skeered de bigger creeturs goin' ter nab me, an skin me, an nail up my hide on de door!"

De Witch-Rabbit, she suck back de thick smoke, an she puff it out again. "I'll bring your smartness back, Brer Rabbit. Just you do ez I say."

"I'll do ez you say, Aunt Mammy-Bammy. "I'll do *anything*."

Now de Witch-Rabbit's two red eye-balls stare out throo de dark, an she say, "Der sets a Squirr'l in dat tree. Go fetch dat Squirr'l straight ter me."

Brer Rabbit look up at de tree, an sure enuff, he see de little white tip of a Squirr'l's tail. "Hmmmm . . ." he say ter hisself, "if I can't coax dat Bunny Bushtail down from der, den my smartness is really-truly gone." Wid dat, Brer Rabbit fetched two rocks. Den he empty out de bag dat Mrs. Rabbit gave him, an he put it on over his head. Den, he sot down under de tree, an he hit de rocks tergedder . . . *blup!*

De Squirr'l, he sing out, "What's dat?"

Brer Rabbit, he don't say nothin'. He slap de rocks tergedder . . . *blap!*

De Squirr'l, he run down de tree a bit, an holler, "Hey! Who's der?"

Brer Rabbit, he don't say nothin'. He just plop de rocks tergedder . . . *blop!*

De Squirr'l, he come down a little furder, an he holler, "Speak up! Who is it?"

"It's Brer Rabbit."

"Brer Rabbit!" say de Squirr'l. "Well, what you doin' der inside dat bag?"

"I'm crackin' hick'ry nuts."

"Hick'ry nuts! Mm . . . mmm . . . mmmm! May I crack some too, Brer Rabbit?"

"Sure enuff, Brer Bushtail. Come on down, an get in dis here bag wid me."

Well suh, de Squirr'l, he come down, an before you could say *hoppagrass,* he wuz inside

88

dat bag, an Brer Rabbit wuz out! An before you could say *hoppapappagrass*, Brer Rabbit wuz luggin' de bag, wid de Squirr'l in it, back ter de hole wher de Witch-Rabbit lived.

Aunt Mammy-Bammy Big-Money hear him comin', an poke her ears up outer de smoke. "Well done, Brer Rabbit, well done!" She reach out fer de bag, an open it, an she let de Squirr'l loose.

"What'll I do now, Aunt Mammy-Bammy?" ask Brer Rabbit.

"Somethin' hard dis time, Brer Rabbit. Der lies a Snake in mongst de grass. Go fetch him here, an fetch him fast."

Now de mawnin' sun wuz bringin' up some light ter see wid, an Brer Rabbit start searchin' round throo de grass. Purty soon, he hear a hissin' in de bushes. Der lay a monstus big Rattlesnake all quiled up! Brer Rabbit jump back. He skeered.

De Snake, he hear him, an he see him. He quile up a little tighter, an he glare at Brer Rabbit wid his tiny, shiny eyes.

Brer Rabbit so skeered he wanter run away, but he walk right up ter dat Snake like he wuzn't skeered at all. "Howdy, Mr. Snake!" he say. "Just fancy meetin' you here like dis! Why, only yestiddy, Brer Bear an me wuz talkin' about you,

sayin' dat you wuz mighty purty when you wuz stretched out full length in de sun. Den we got ter arguin' about how long you is. Brer Bear, he say you ain't but three foot long . . . but me, I say you is four."

De Snake, he don't say nothin', but he swell up a little, like he feelin' proud.

Brer Rabbit, he speak up, real perlite, "Mr. Snake, I'd like ter ask a favor. Would you be so kind ez ter onquile yourself, an let me measure you, so's ter settle dat argument 'twixt me an Brer Bear?"

Well . . . Mr. Snake he wanter show off how long he is, so purty soon, he onquile, an stretch out.

Now Brer Rabbit reach inter his pocket an pull out a piece of string. He step up close ter de Snake like he goin' ter measure . . . but he don't measure. He slip dat string round dat Snake's fat neck. *Trrpp!* . . . he yank it! Now Mr. Snake wuz tied up tight. He hiss an he rattle, an he whip around, but he can't get loose from dat string.

Brer Rabbit drag him along throo de grass,

back ter wher de Witch-Rabbit wuz waitin' in de smoke.

"Well done, Brer Rabbit, well done!" she say. Den she grab Mr. Snake an she fling him way off somewhers, so's he can't come back.

"What'll I do now, Aunty Mammy-Bammy?" ask Brer Rabbit.

"Dis time," she say, "you got ter do somethin' *really* hard. In de forest, an Elephent roams about. Go fetch me a tusk from out his snout."

"A ELEPHENT-TUSK!" Brer Rabbit's mouf drop open wide, an he stand stock still, like he wuz turned inter stone. "Why, I ain't never e'en laid eyes on a Elephent! He's de biggest creetur on dis earf!"

"Don't argue wid me, Brer Rabbit! You said you'd do *anything!* But of course, maybe you ain't smart enuff ter fetch a Elephent tusk. In dat case, I'll ask Brer Fox ter fetch it."

"Oh no, Aunt Mammy-Bammy, not Brer Fox! I'll fetch it! I'll fetch it right now!"

Wid dat, Brer Rabbit hop off. An he don't stop hoppin' day or night, till he get all de long way ter de forest. Den, when he finally got der, he climbed up in a tree ter wait fer a Elephent ter come by.

After a while, he hear a heavy tromp-tromp an a crashin' an smashin' of trees. Along come

Brer Elephent, big ez a house. He wuz floppin' his great ears, an swingin' his long danglin' snout.

Brer Rabbit sot der in de tree, an he wuz skeered well-nigh ter deff. Howsomever, he sing out, "Howdy!"

De Elephent don't answer. He just stand der, switchin' his snout from side ter side.

Brer Rabbit, he sing out again. "Say, Brer Elephent, is it true what I heard King Lion sayin' down at de spring? He say you is too big ter be very strong."

"Haw haw!" snort de Elephent. "Me not strong? Watch dis!" He fling out his snout, an he pull off de branch of a poplar tree, an toss it away.

"Pshaw!" say Brer Rabbit. "Dat wuz easy."

"Easy?" say de Elephent. "Well den...watch dis!" Now he swing his snout real low, an he pull up de whole poplar tree, root an all. Den he flip it up inter de air, like 'twurn't nothin' more dan a fedder duster.

"Shucks!" say Brer Rabbit. "Dat really wuzn't

much of a tree!" Now he point ter an enormous ole pine tree, wid a trunk ez big ez Brer Elephent hisself. "I'll bet you ain't strong enuff ter knock *dat* down!"

"I ain't?" Now de Elephent mad. "Watch me *dis* time!" he holler. Wid dat, he start-a-runnin', an he crash inter dat enormous pine tree *kerblashity blam!* De pine tree, it don't budge, but Brer Elephent's tusk, it smack against de tree trunk, an *Crack!* it break off!

"Ow! Ow!" beller Brer Elephent. An whiles he wuz standin' der ow-owin', Brer Rabbit skittle up. He grab de big tusk, and drag it away.

He drag it all de way back ter de Witch-Rabbit's hole. "Here I am, Aunt Mammy-Bammy Big-Money!" he yell down inter de smoke. "I fetched de Elephent tusk like you told me! What do you want me ter do now next?"

Fer a minute, de Witch-Rabbit don't answer. Den her voice come floatin' up from way down yonder below. "I don't want you ter do nothin' at all. An don't you worry no more about losin' your smartness. If you wuz any smarter dan you is right now, you'd be de ruination of de whole wide wurld."

Den Brer Rabbit feel mighty, mighty good. He drag de Elephent tusk home ter Mrs. Rabbit, an he tell her dat now, an forever more, he done got over de mopes.

So Brer Rabbit started right in playin' pranks again, an he ain't never stopped from dat day down ter dis. An ter-day, when folks go strollin' throo de woods, if dey lissen real sharp, dey can hear ole Brer Rabbit prancin' round, pokin' his nose inter some new mischief, chucklin', laffin', an cuttin' up fit ter kill.